nickelodeon

TEENAGE MUTANT NINJA TURTLES™

AMAZING ADVENTURES

VOLUME 4

nickelodeon

IDW

Become our fan on Facebook facebook.com/idwpublishing
Follow us on Twitter @idwpublishing
Subscribe to us on YouTube youtube.com/idwpublishing
See what's new on Tumblr tumblr.idwpublishing.com
Check us out on Instagram instagram.com/idwpublsing

ISBN: 978-1-63140-843-4 20 19 18 17 2 3 4 5

COVER BY
JON SOMMARIVA

COLLECTION EDITS BY
JUSTIN EISINGER
AND ALONZO SIMON

COLLECTION DESIGN BY
RON ESTEVEZ

PUBLISHER
TED ADAMS

Special Thanks to Joan Hilty & Linda Lee for their invaluable assistance.

Originally published as TEENAGE MUTANT NINJA TURTLES: AMAZING ADVENTURES issues #13–14 and TEENAGE MUTANT NINJA TURTLES: AMAZING ADVENTURES: CARMELO ANTHONY SPECIAL ONE-SHOT.

For international rights, please
contact licensing@idwpublishing.com

THE DRIP
STORY BY MATTHEW K. MANNING
ART BY CHAD THOMAS
COLORS BY HEATHER BRECKEL

INSTRU-MENTAL
STORY BY CALEB GOELLNER
ART BY BUSTER MOODY
COLORS BY HEATHER BRECKEL
COLOR ASSIST BY LUDWIG LAGUNA OLIMBA

REMEMBER THAT ONE TIME...?
STORY BY MATTHEW K. MANNING
ART BY JON SOMMARIVA
COLORS BY LEONARDO ITO

CARMELO ANTHONY SPECIAL
STORY BY MATTHEW K. MANNING
ART BY CHAD THOMAS
COLORS BY HEATHER BRECKEL

LETTERS BY SHAWN LEE
SERIES EDITS BY BOBBY CURNOW

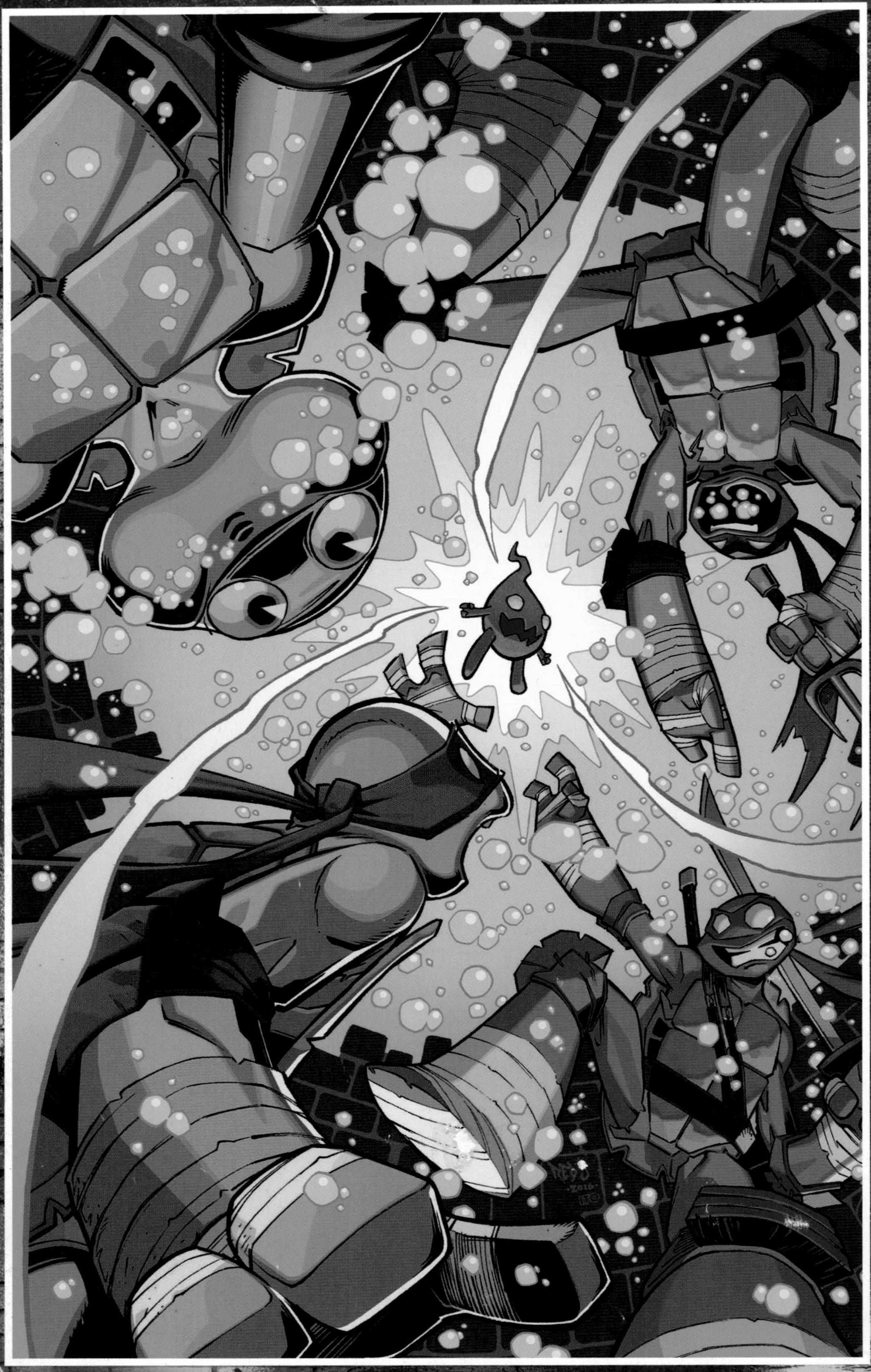

THE DRIP

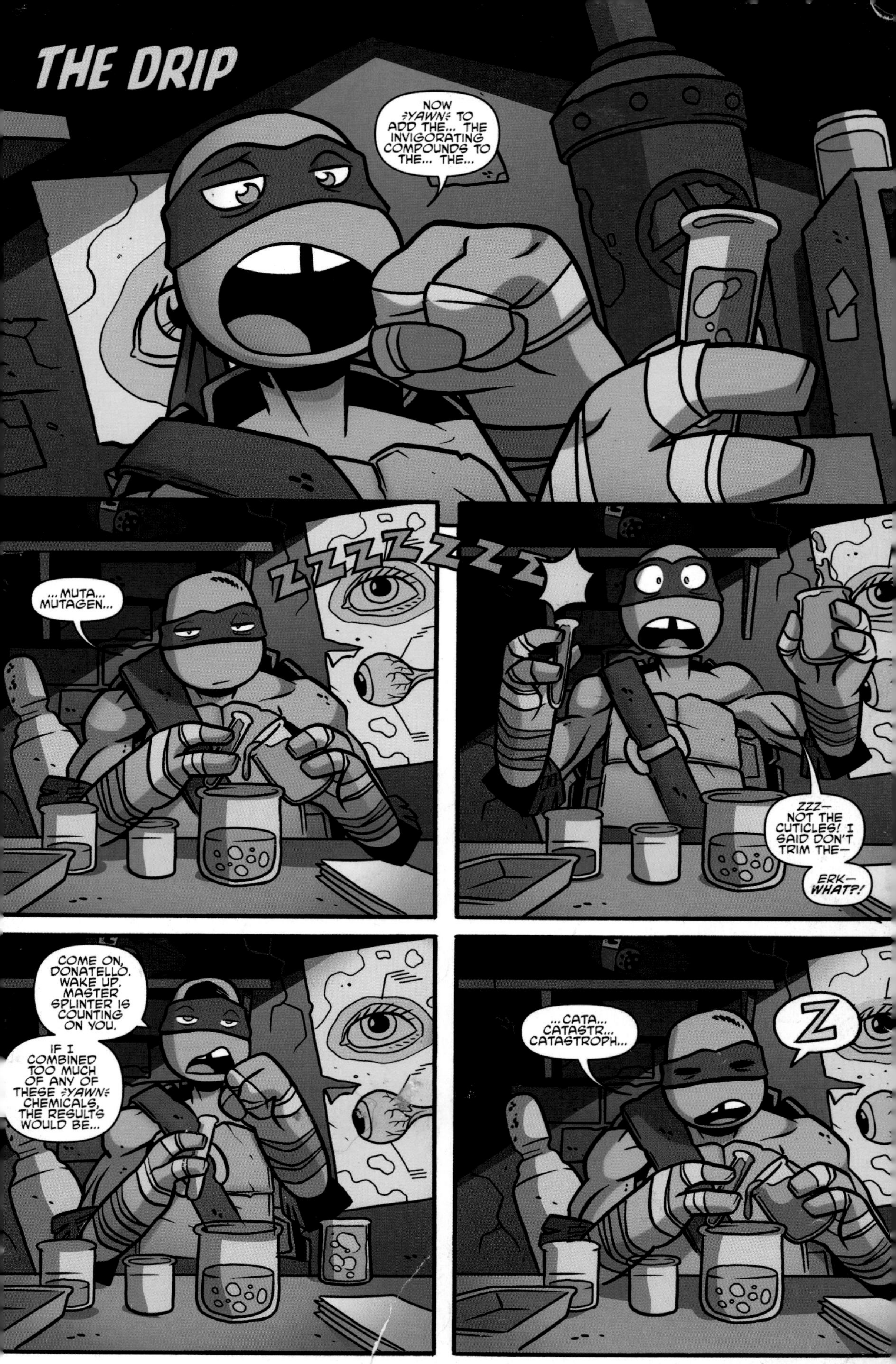

NOW *YAWN* TO ADD THE... THE INVIGORATING COMPOUNDS TO THE... THE...
...MUTA... MUTAGEN...
ZZZZZZZZZ
ZZZ— NOT THE CUTICLES! I SAID DON'T TRIM THE—
ERK— WHAT?!
COME ON, DONATELLO. WAKE UP. MASTER SPLINTER IS COUNTING ON YOU.
IF I COMBINED TOO MUCH OF ANY OF THESE *YAWN* CHEMICALS, THE RESULTS WOULD BE...
...CATA... CATASTR... CATASTROPH...
Z

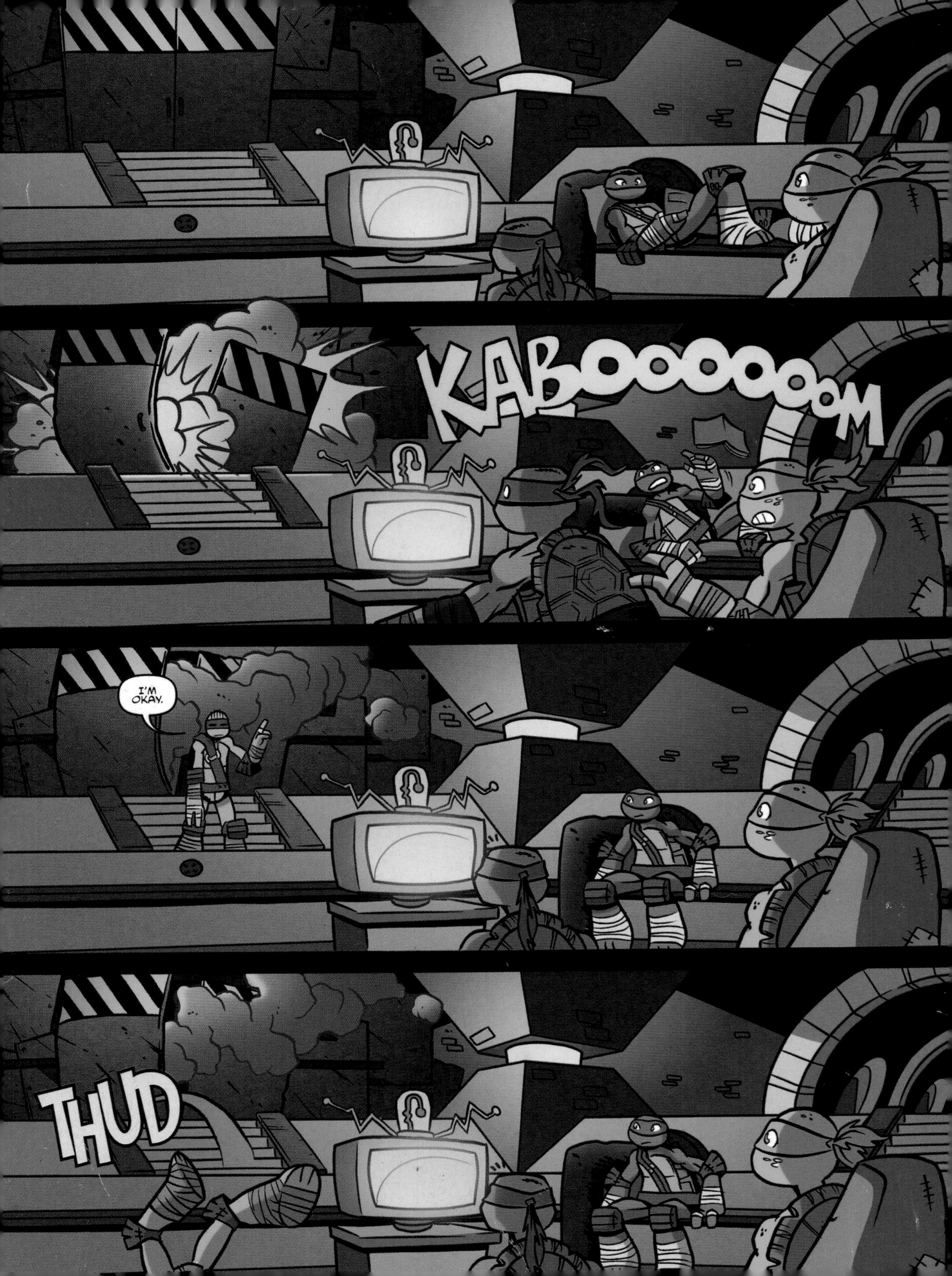
KABOOOOOOOM
I'M OKAY.
THUD

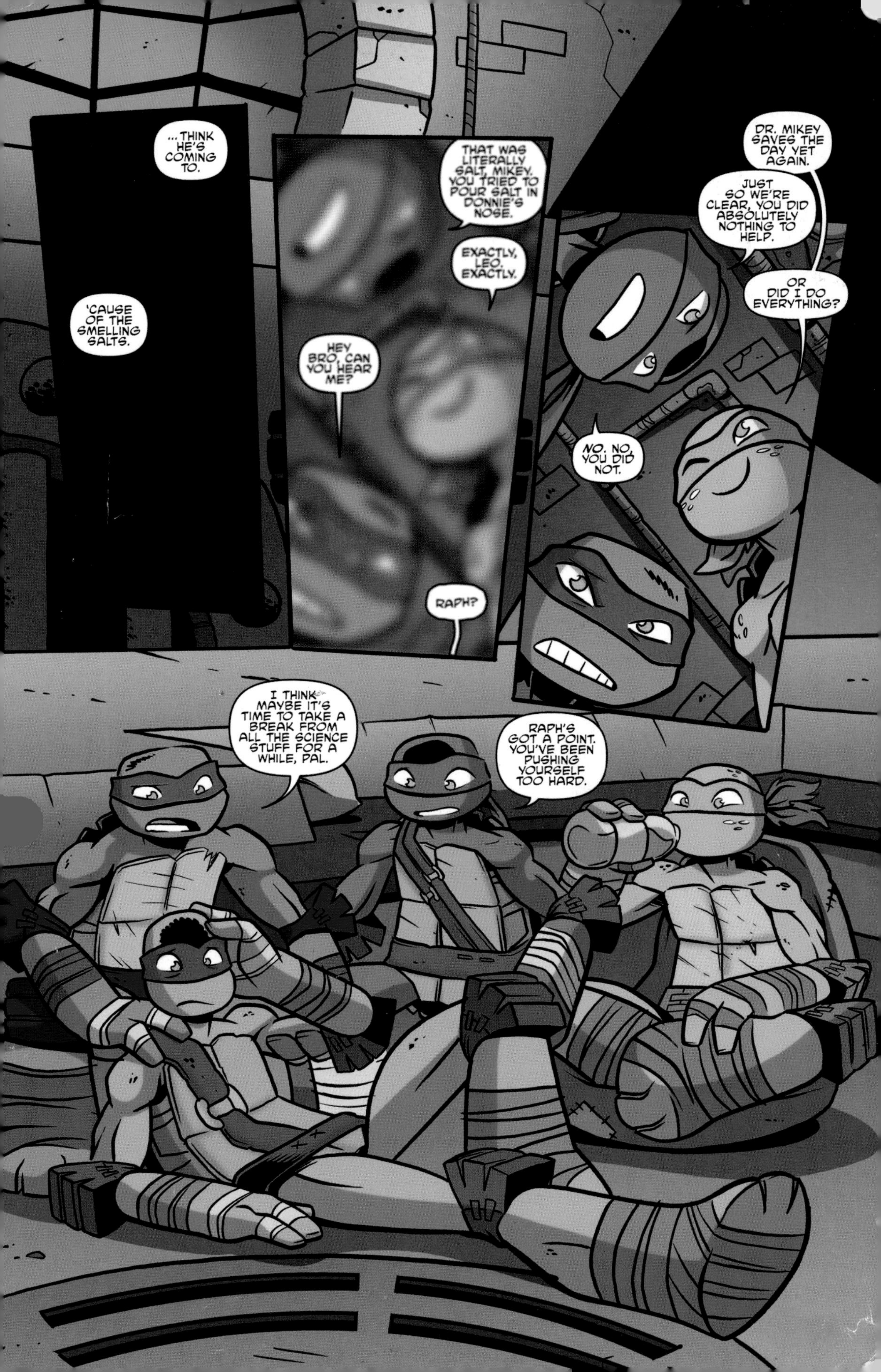
...THINK HE'S COMING TO.
'CAUSE OF THE SMELLING SALTS.
THAT WAS LITERALLY SALT, MIKEY. YOU TRIED TO POUR SALT IN DONNIE'S NOSE.
EXACTLY, LEO. EXACTLY.
HEY BRO, CAN YOU HEAR ME?
RAPH?
DR. MIKEY SAVES THE DAY YET AGAIN.
JUST SO WE'RE CLEAR, YOU DID ABSOLUTELY NOTHING TO HELP.
OR DID I DO EVERYTHING?
NO. NO, YOU DID NOT.
I THINK MAYBE IT'S TIME TO TAKE A BREAK FROM ALL THE SCIENCE STUFF FOR A WHILE, PAL.
RAPH'S GOT A POINT. YOU'VE BEEN PUSHING YOURSELF TOO HARD.

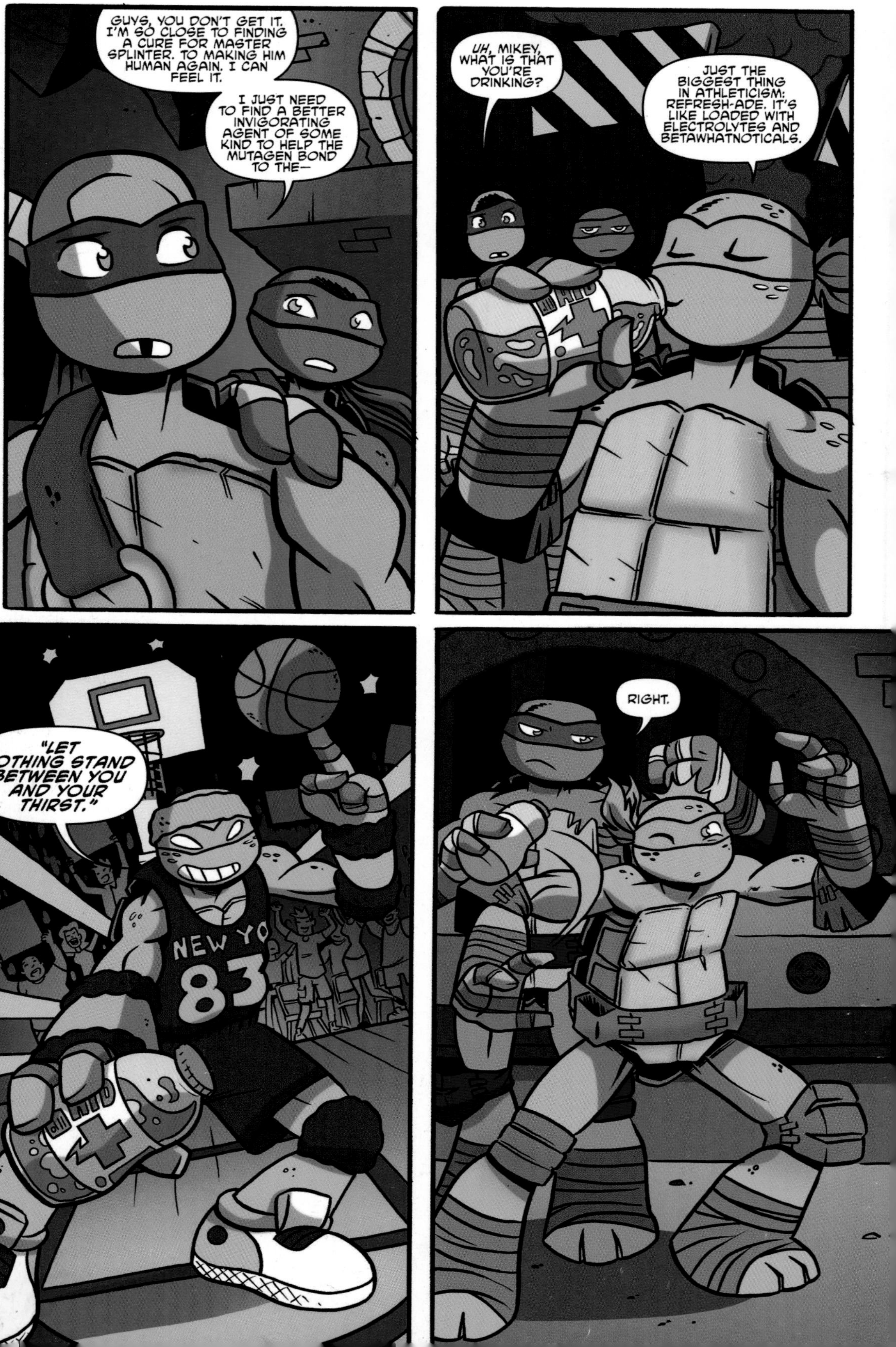
GUYS, YOU DON'T GET IT. I'M SO CLOSE TO FINDING A CURE FOR MASTER SPLINTER. TO MAKING HIM HUMAN AGAIN. I CAN FEEL IT.
I JUST NEED TO FIND A BETTER INVIGORATING AGENT OF SOME KIND TO HELP THE MUTAGEN BOND TO THE—
UH, MIKEY, WHAT IS THAT YOU'RE DRINKING?
JUST THE BIGGEST THING IN ATHLETICISM: REFRESH-ADE. IT'S LIKE LOADED WITH ELECTROLYTES AND BETAWHATNOTICALS.
"LET NOTHING STAND BETWEEN YOU AND YOUR THIRST."
NEW YO
83
RIGHT.

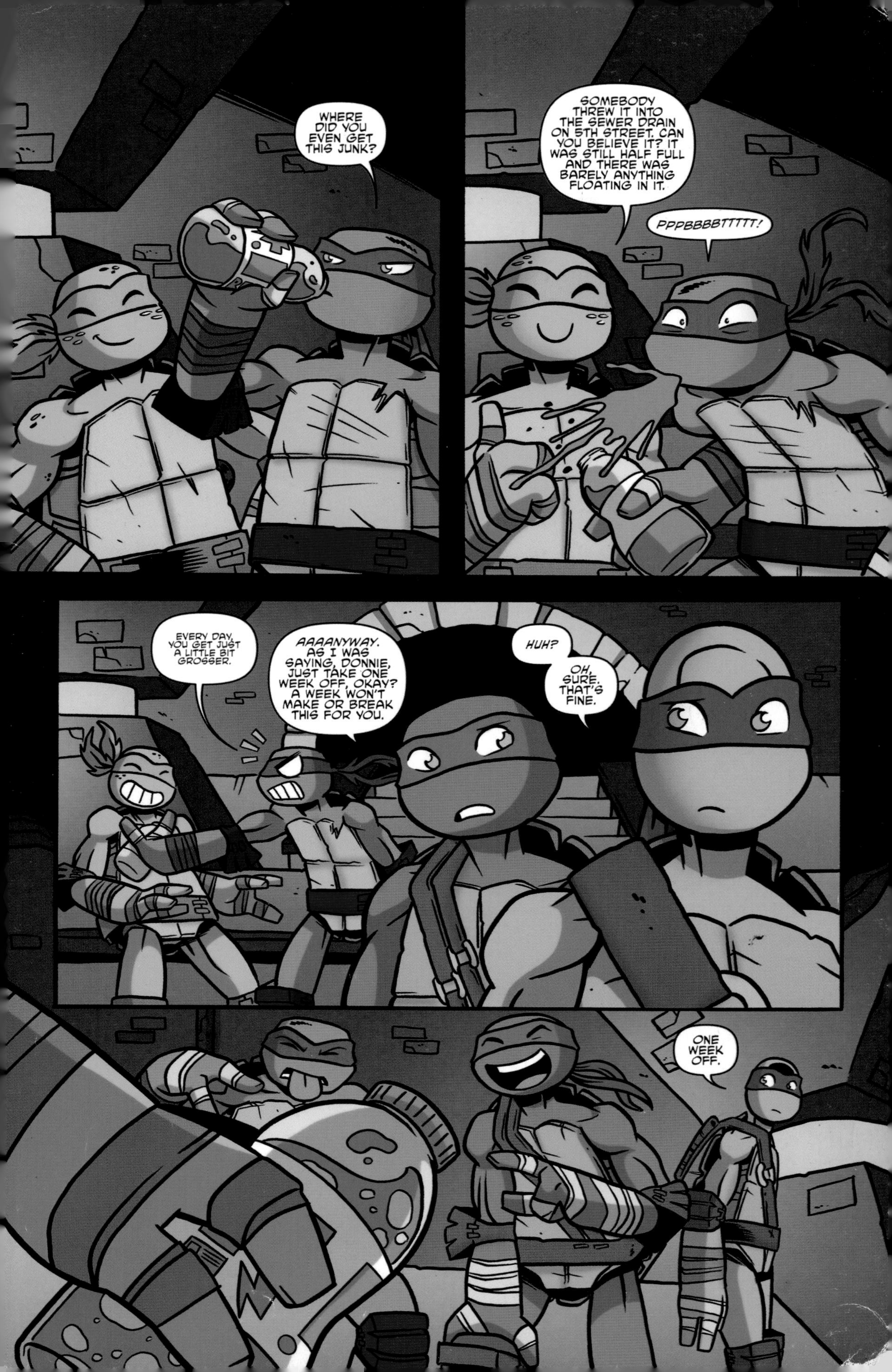
WHERE DID YOU EVEN GET THIS JUNK?
SOMEBODY THREW IT INTO THE SEWER DRAIN ON 5TH STREET. CAN YOU BELIEVE IT? IT WAS STILL HALF FULL AND THERE WAS BARELY ANYTHING FLOATING IN IT.
PPPBBBBTTTTT!
EVERY DAY, YOU GET JUST A LITTLE BIT GROSSER.
AAAANYWAY. AS I WAS SAYING, DONNIE, JUST TAKE ONE WEEK OFF, OKAY? A WEEK WON'T MAKE OR BREAK THIS FOR YOU.
HUH?
OH, SURE. THAT'S FINE.
ONE WEEK OFF.

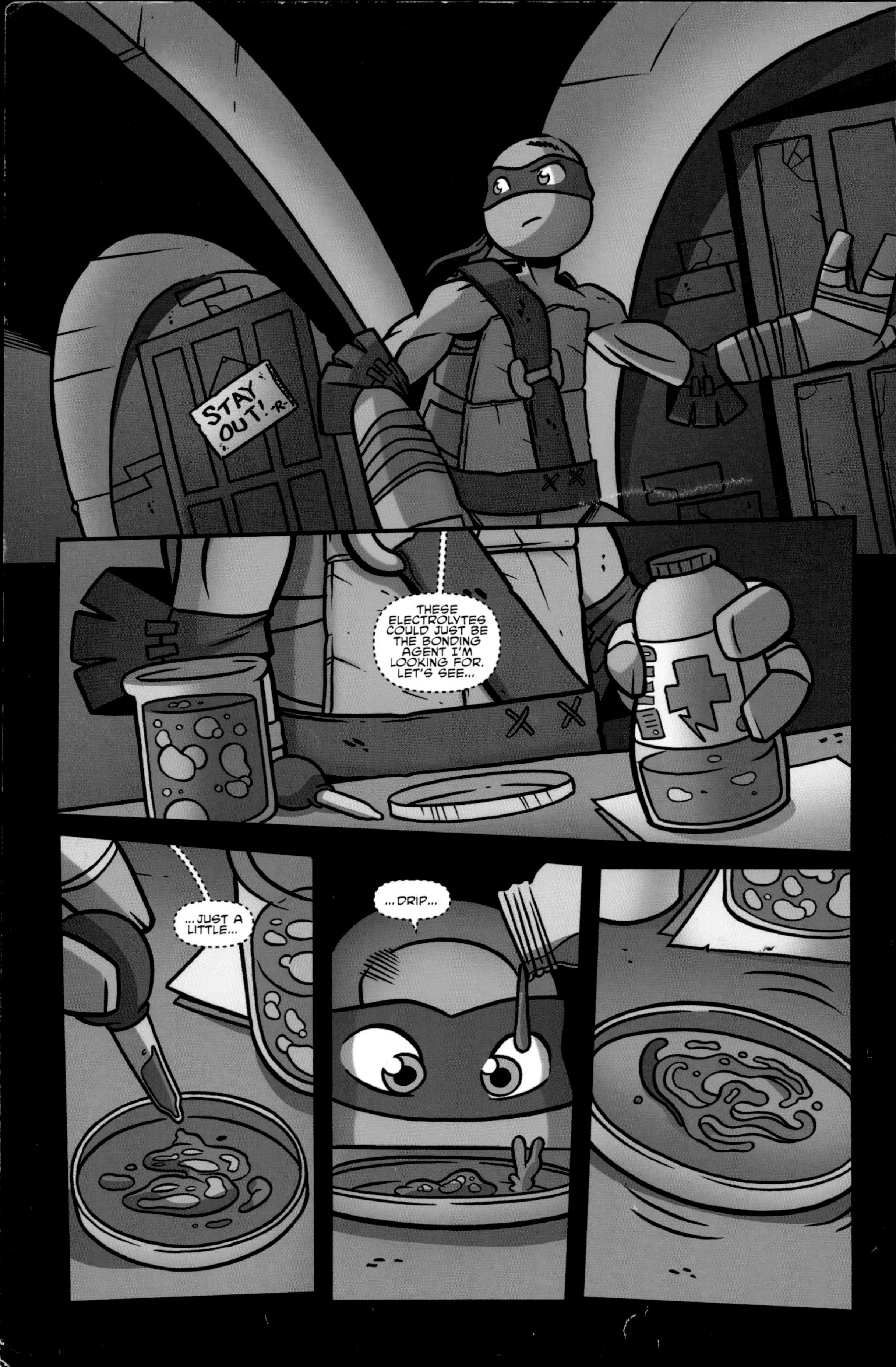
STAY OUT! -R-
THESE ELECTROLYTES COULD JUST BE THE BONDING AGENT I'M LOOKING FOR. LET'S SEE...
...JUST A LITTLE...
...DRIP...

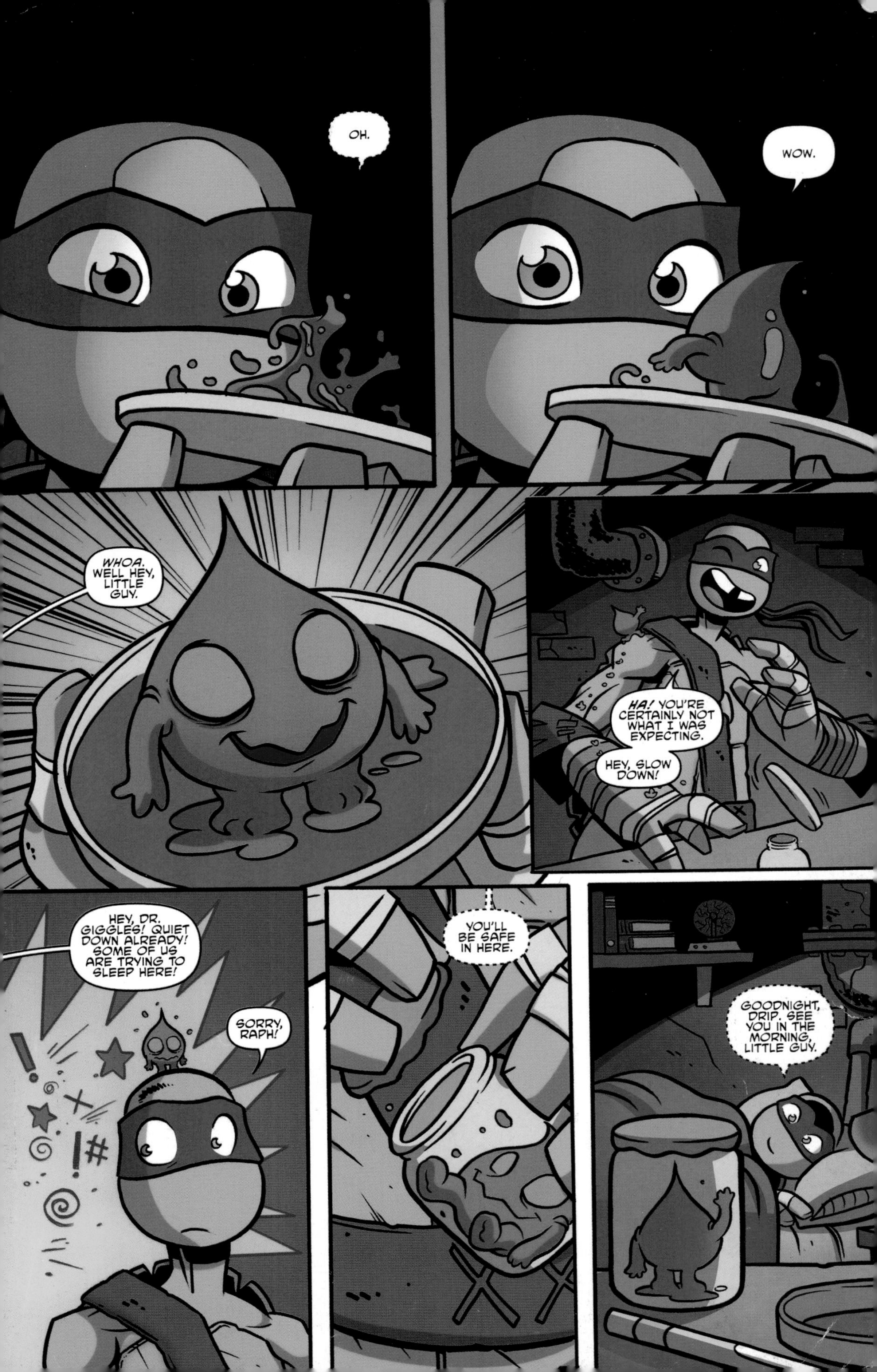

OH.
WOW.
WHOA. WELL HEY, LITTLE GUY.
HA! YOU'RE CERTAINLY NOT WHAT I WAS EXPECTING.
HEY, SLOW DOWN!
HEY, DR. GIGGLES! QUIET DOWN ALREADY! SOME OF US ARE TRYING TO SLEEP HERE!
SORRY, RAPH!
YOU'LL BE SAFE IN HERE.
GOODNIGHT, DRIP. SEE YOU IN THE MORNING, LITTLE GUY.

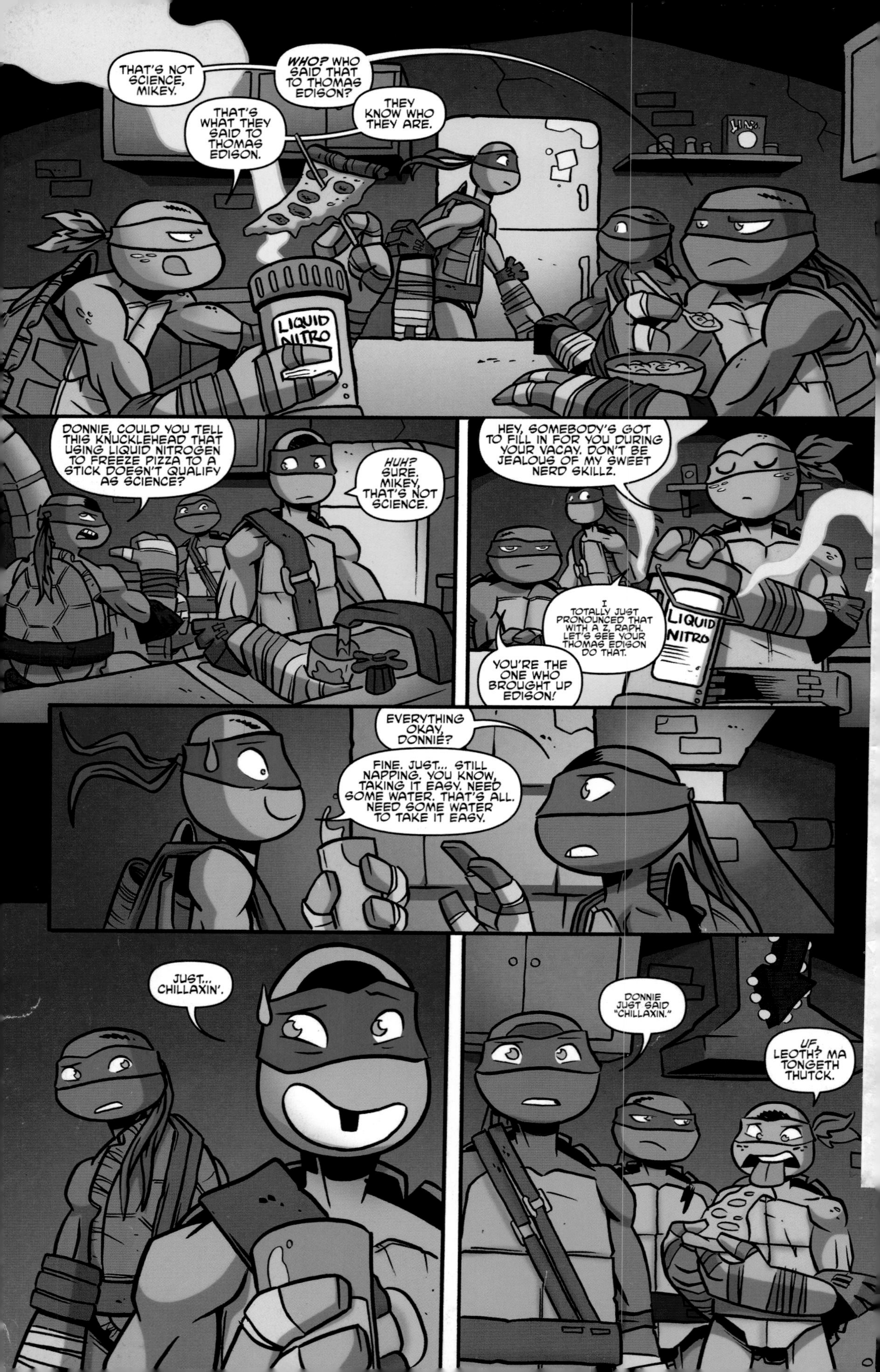

THAT'S NOT SCIENCE, MIKEY.
THAT'S WHAT THEY SAID TO THOMAS EDISON.
WHO? WHO SAID THAT TO THOMAS EDISON?
THEY KNOW WHO THEY ARE.
LIQUID NITRO
DONNIE, COULD YOU TELL THIS KNUCKLEHEAD THAT USING LIQUID NITROGEN TO FREEZE PIZZA TO A STICK DOESN'T QUALIFY AS SCIENCE?
HUH? SURE. MIKEY, THAT'S NOT SCIENCE.
HEY, SOMEBODY'S GOT TO FILL IN FOR YOU DURING YOUR VACAY. DON'T BE JEALOUS OF MY SWEET NERD SKILLZ.
I TOTALLY JUST PRONOUNCED THAT WITH A Z, RAPH. LET'S SEE YOUR THOMAS EDISON DO THAT.
YOU'RE THE ONE WHO BROUGHT UP EDISON!
LIQUID NITRO
EVERYTHING OKAY, DONNIE?
FINE. JUST... STILL NAPPING. YOU KNOW, TAKING IT EASY. NEED SOME WATER. THAT'S ALL. NEED SOME WATER TO TAKE IT EASY.
JUST... CHILLAXIN'.
DONNIE JUST SAID "CHILLAXIN."
UF, LEOTH? MA TONGETH THUTCK.

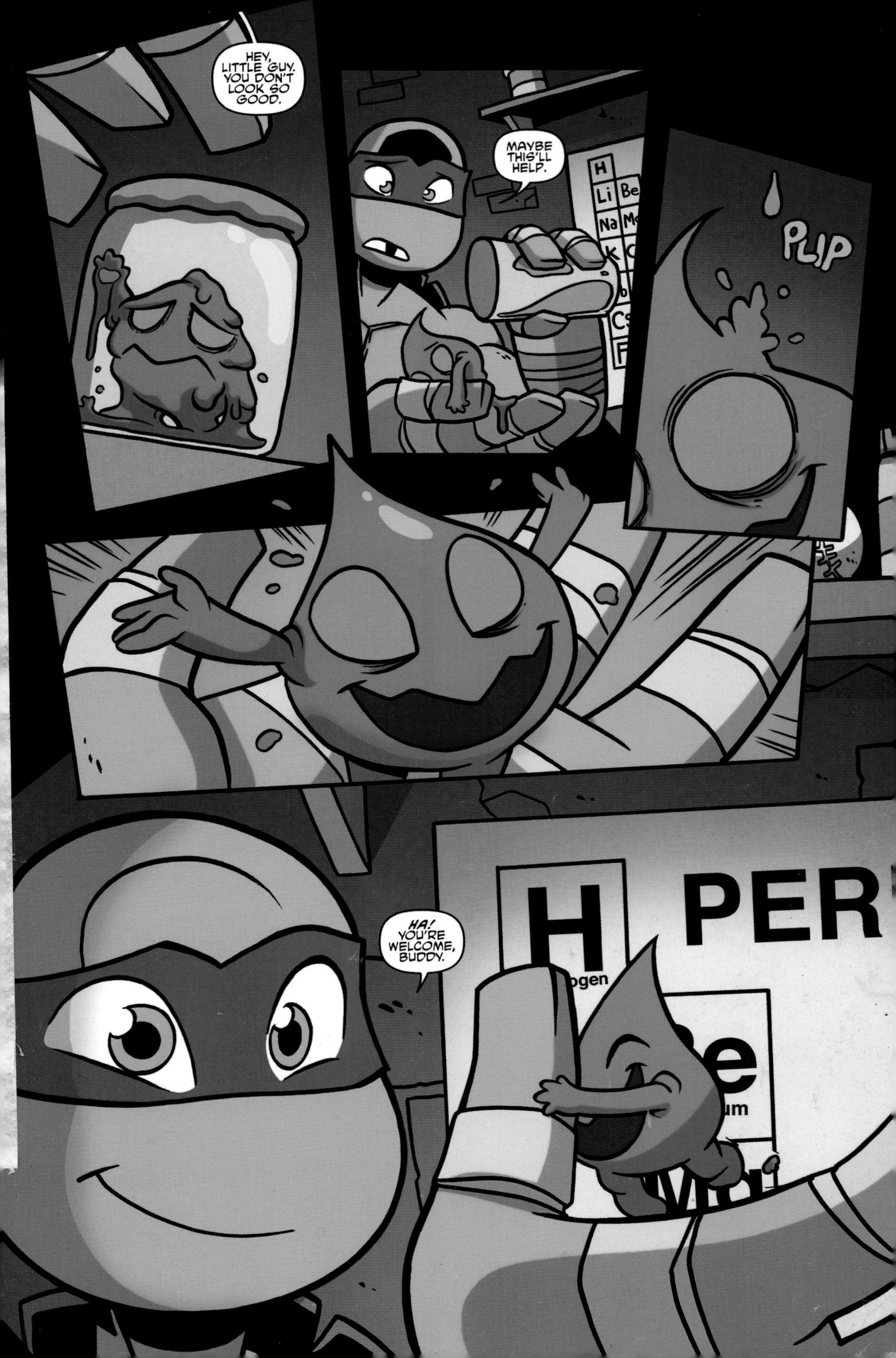

HEY, LITTLE GUY. YOU DON'T LOOK SO GOOD.
MAYBE THIS'LL HELP.
PLIP
HA! YOU'RE WELCOME, BUDDY.

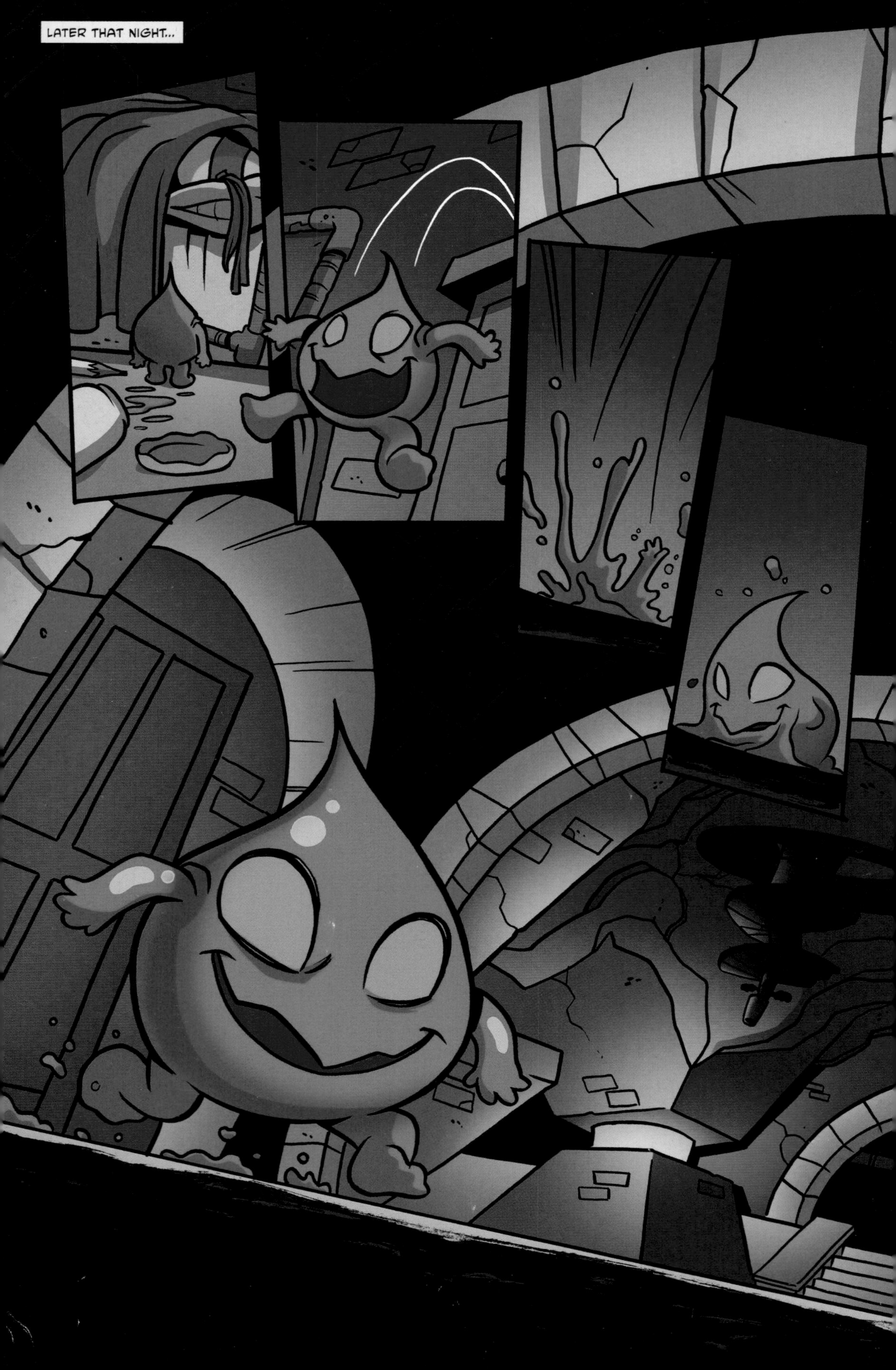
LATER THAT NIGHT...

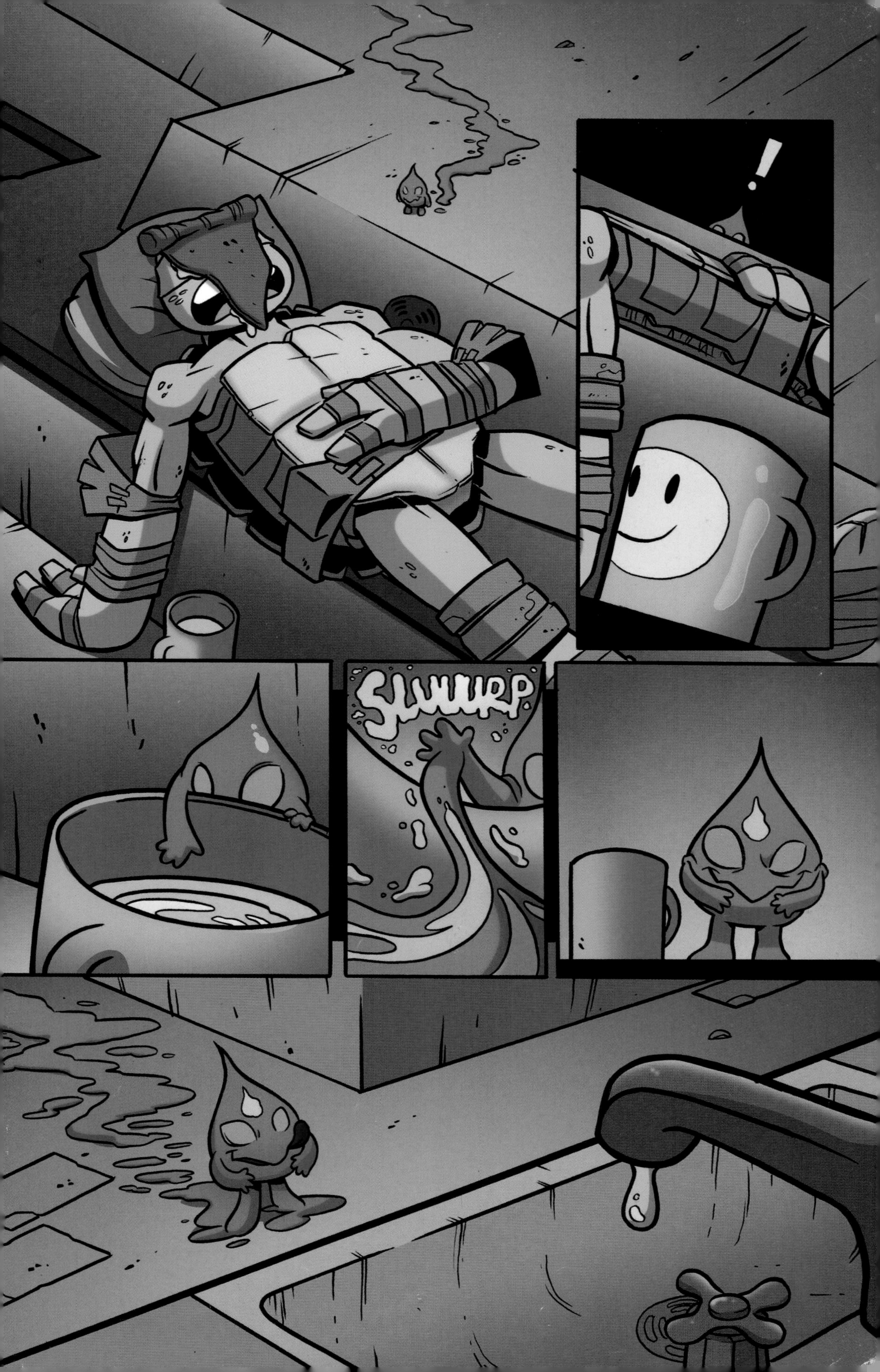
!
SLUUURP

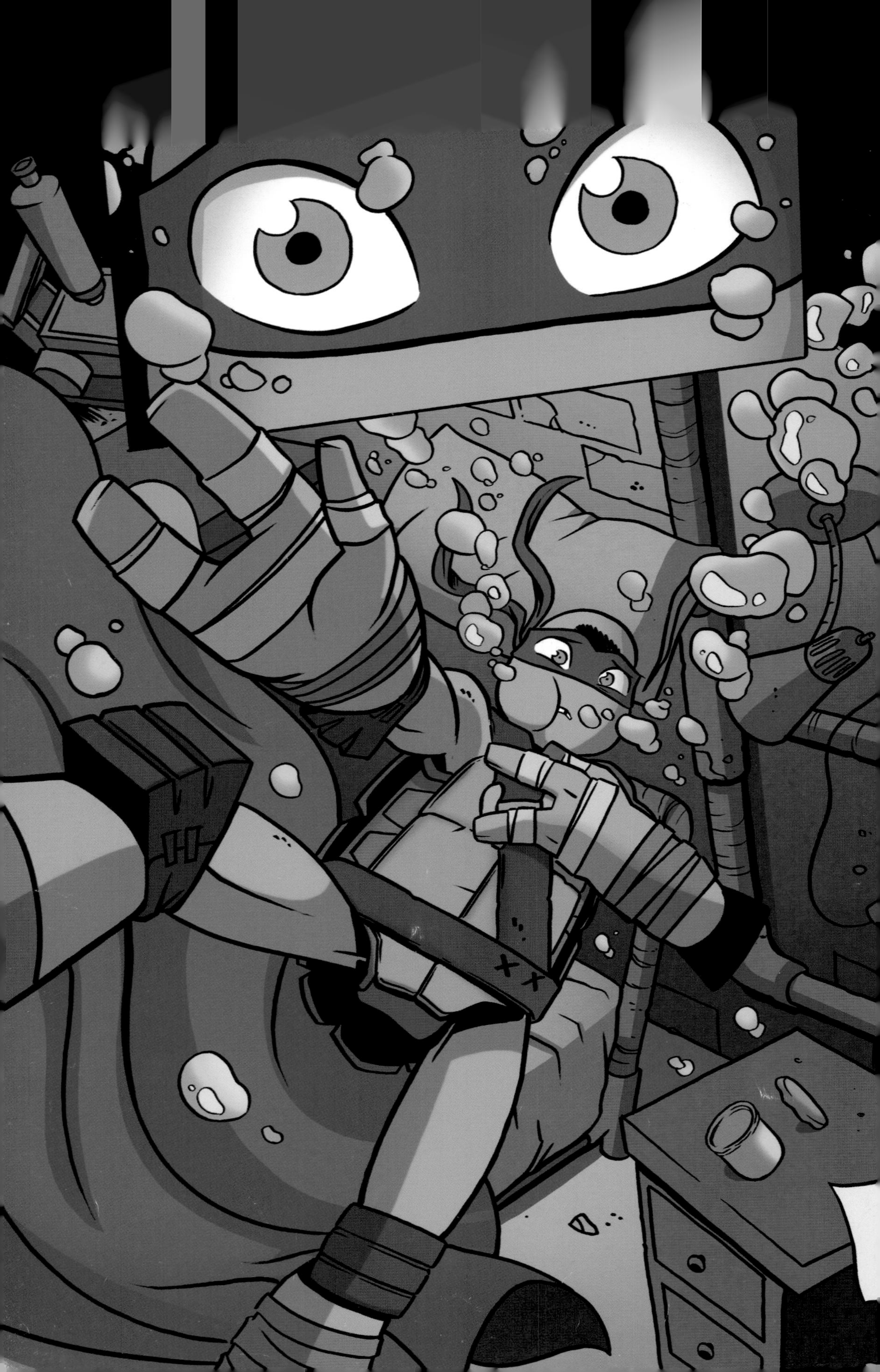

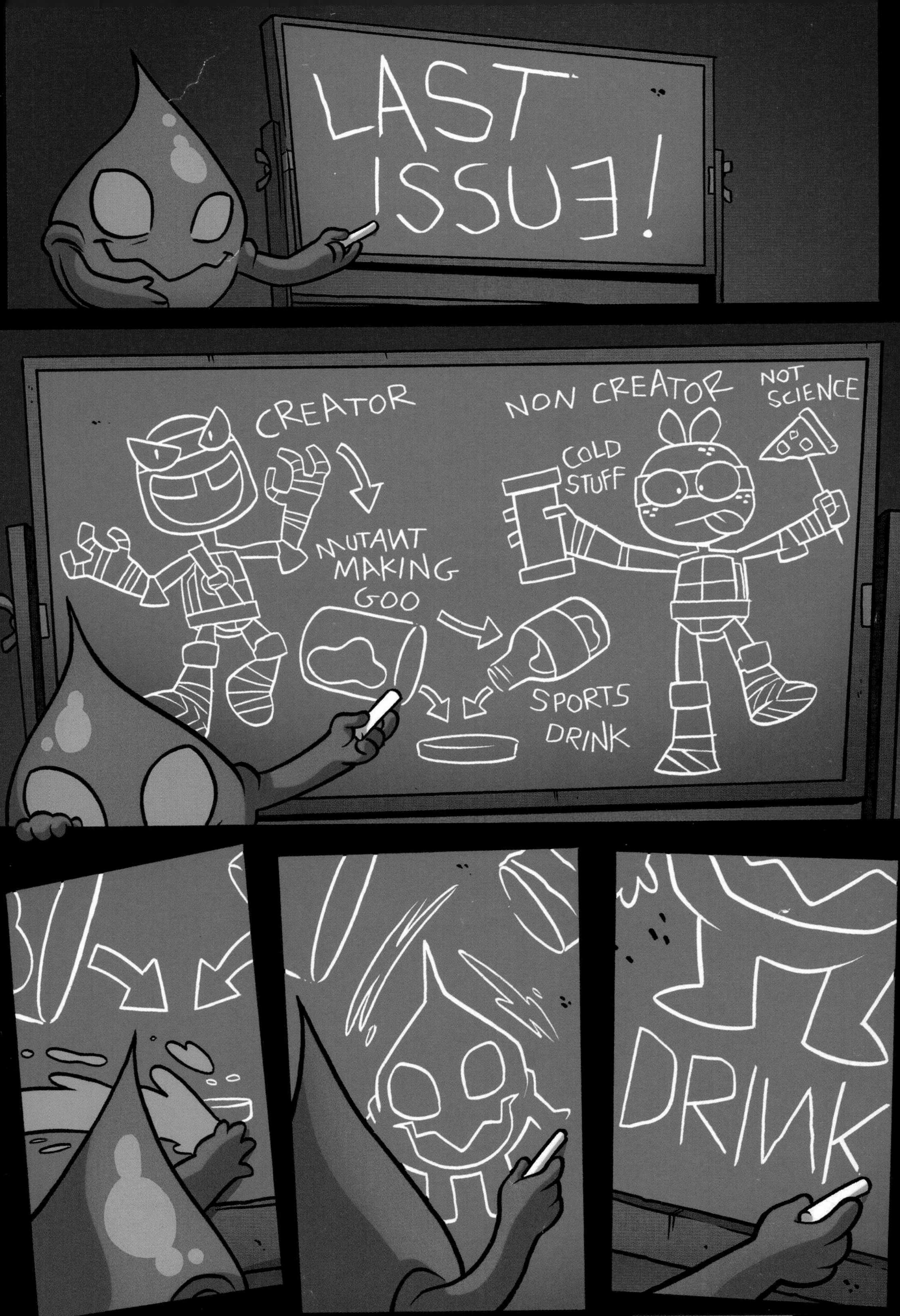
LAST ISSUE!
CREATOR
NON CREATOR
NOT SCIENCE
COLD STUFF
MUTANT MAKING GOO
SPORTS DRINK
DRINK

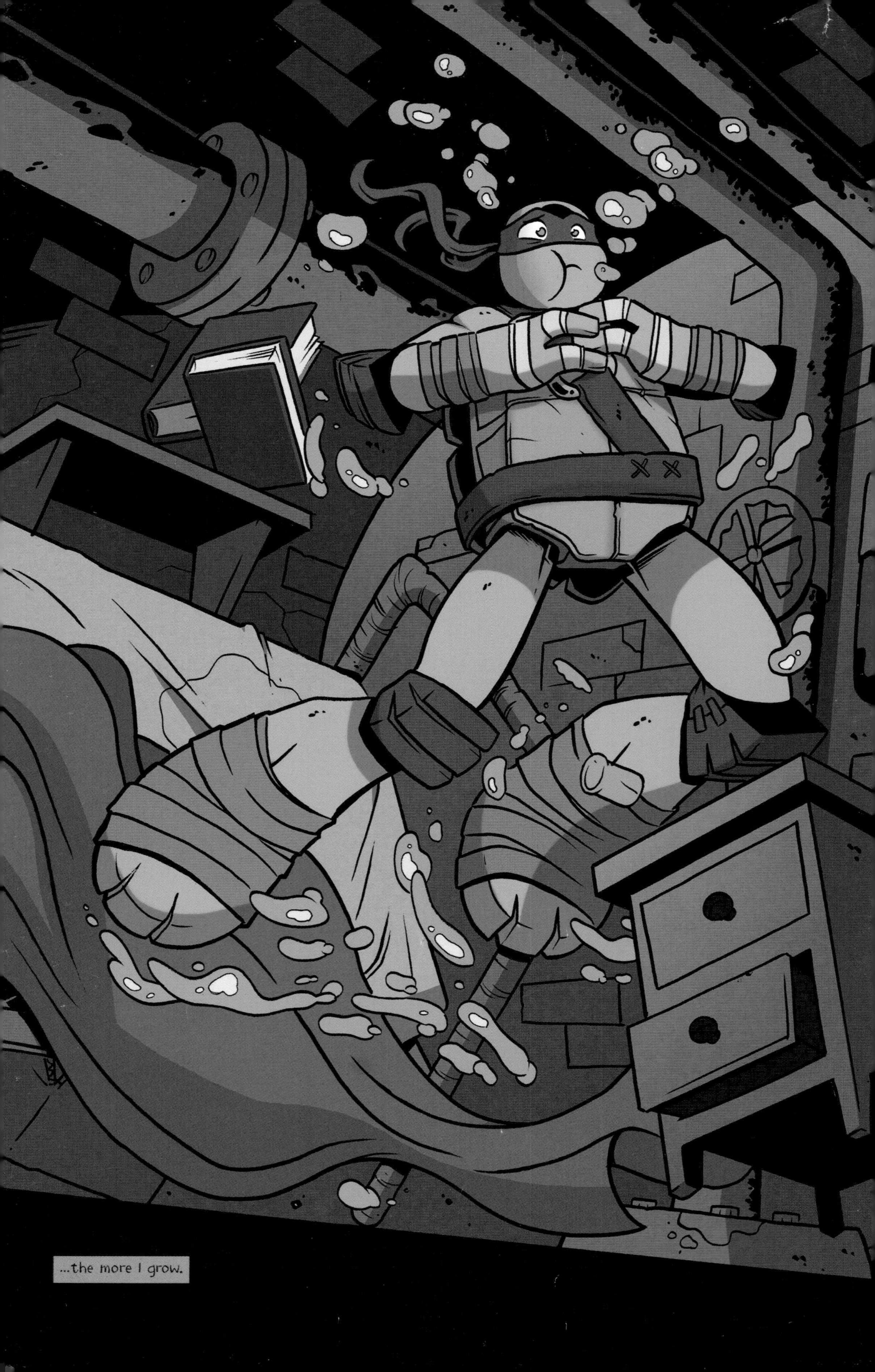
...the more I grow.

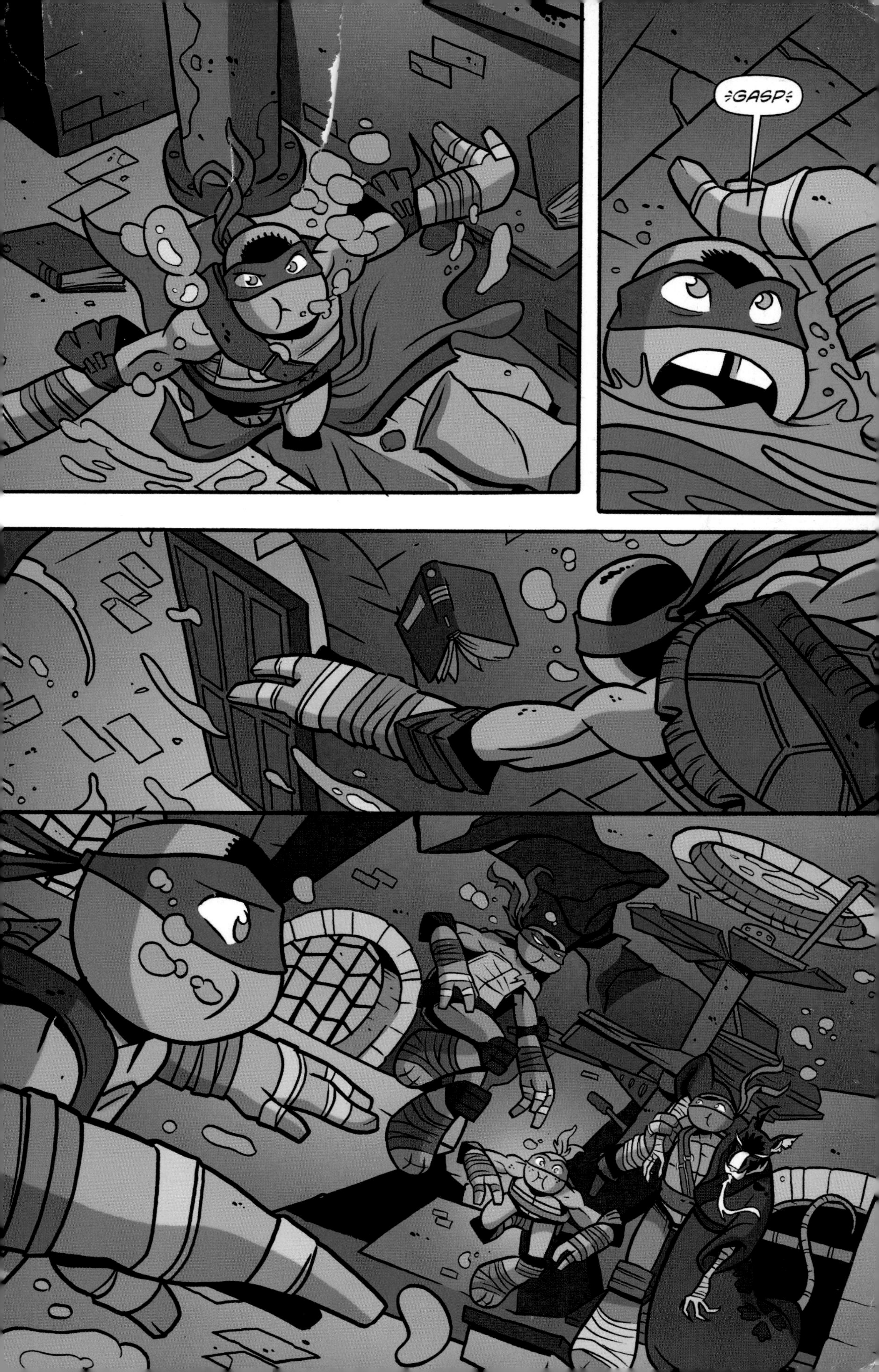
GASP

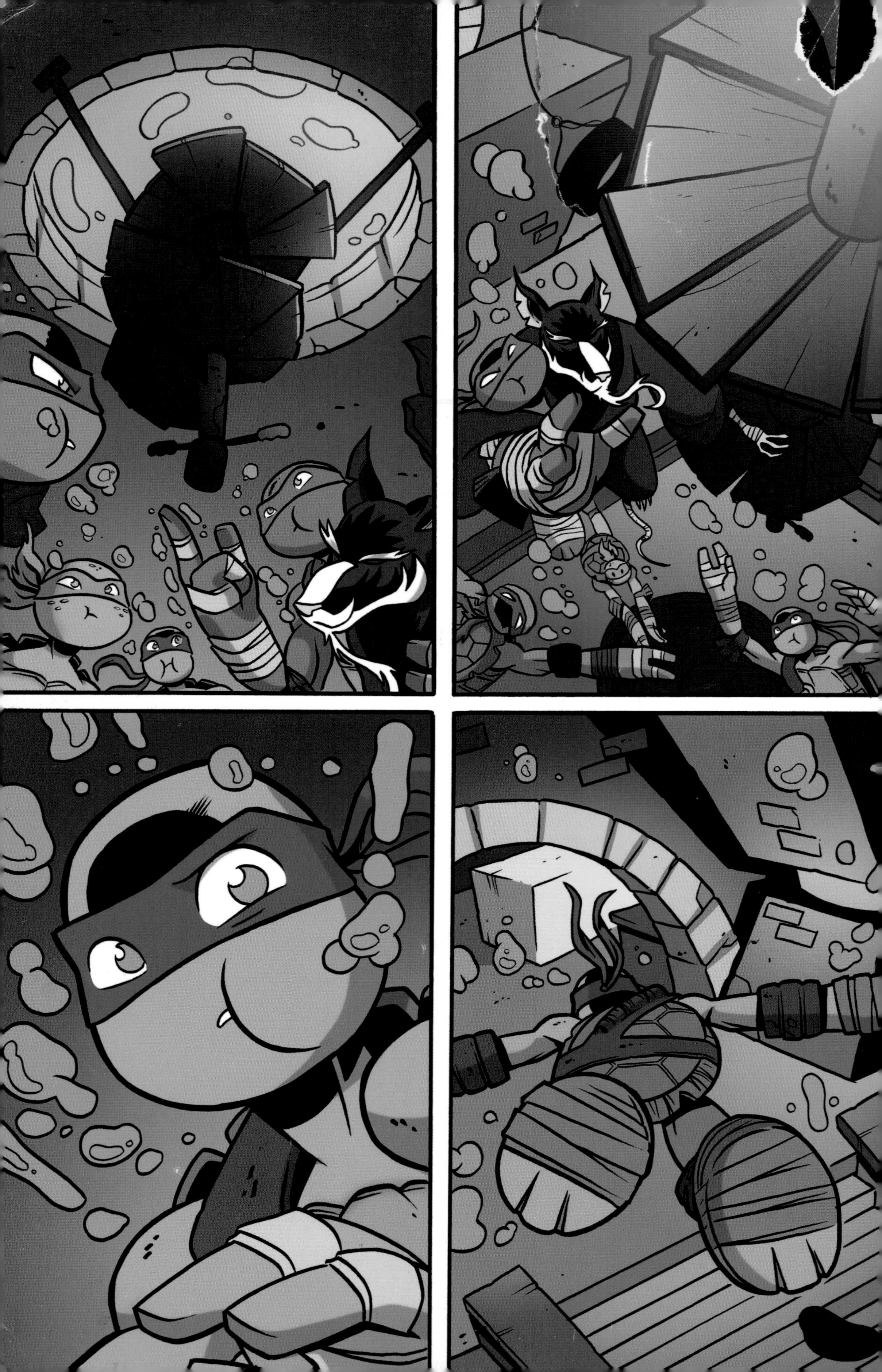

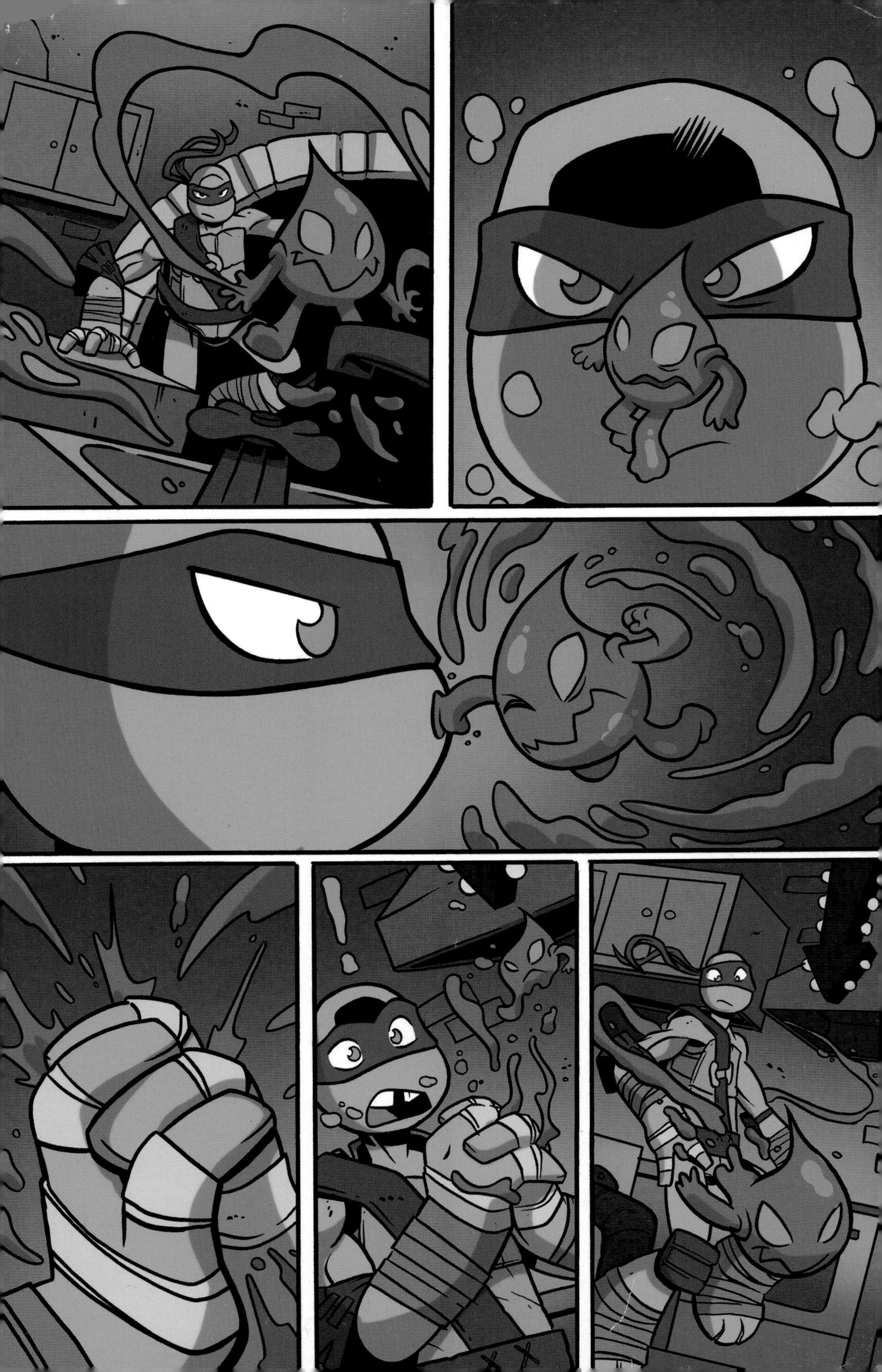

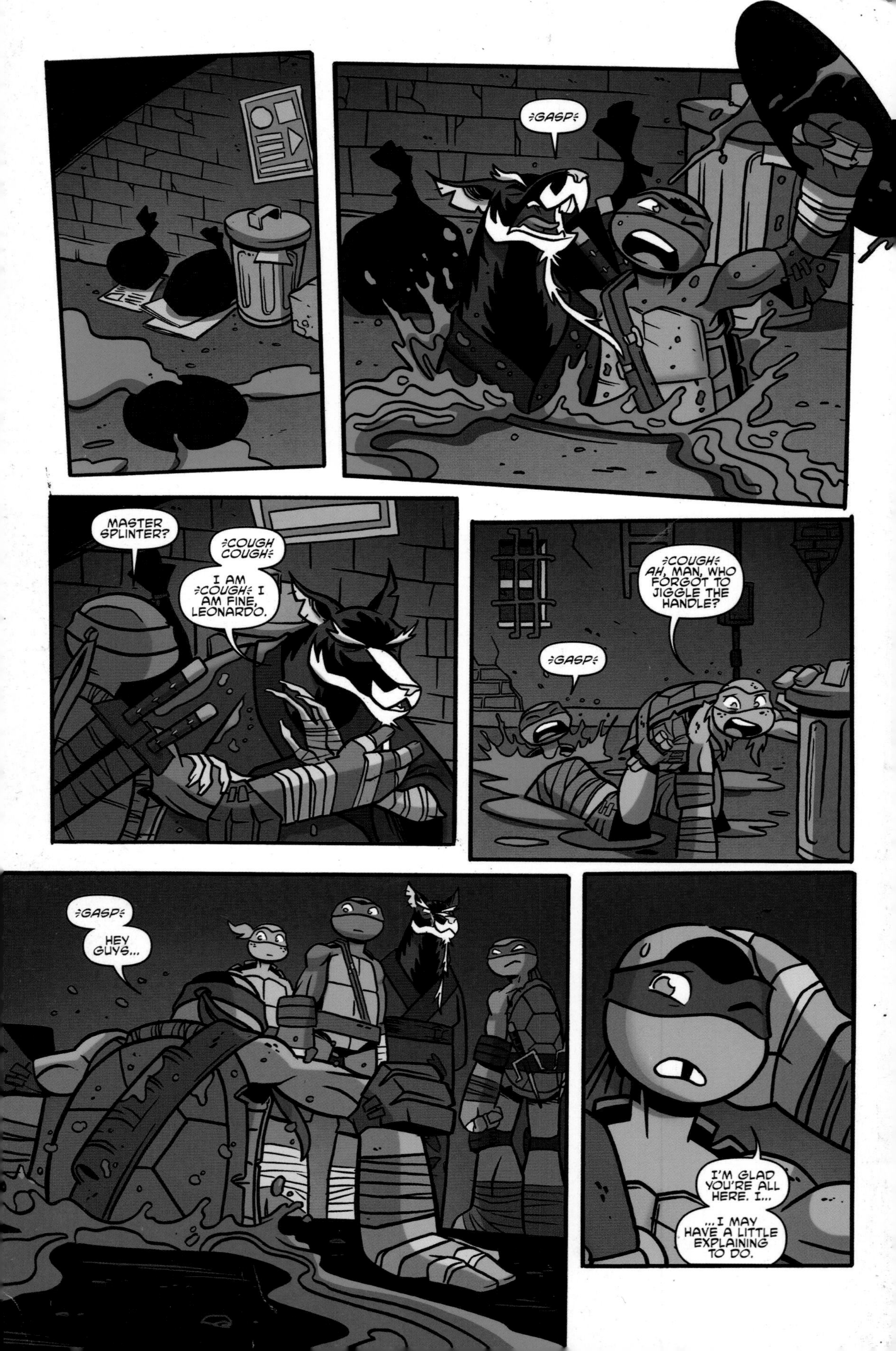

GASP
MASTER SPLINTER?
COUGH COUGH
I AM COUGH I AM FINE, LEONARDO.
COUGH AH, MAN, WHO FORGOT TO JIGGLE THE HANDLE?
GASP
GASP
HEY GUYS...
I'M GLAD YOU'RE ALL HERE. I...
...I MAY HAVE A LITTLE EXPLAINING TO DO.

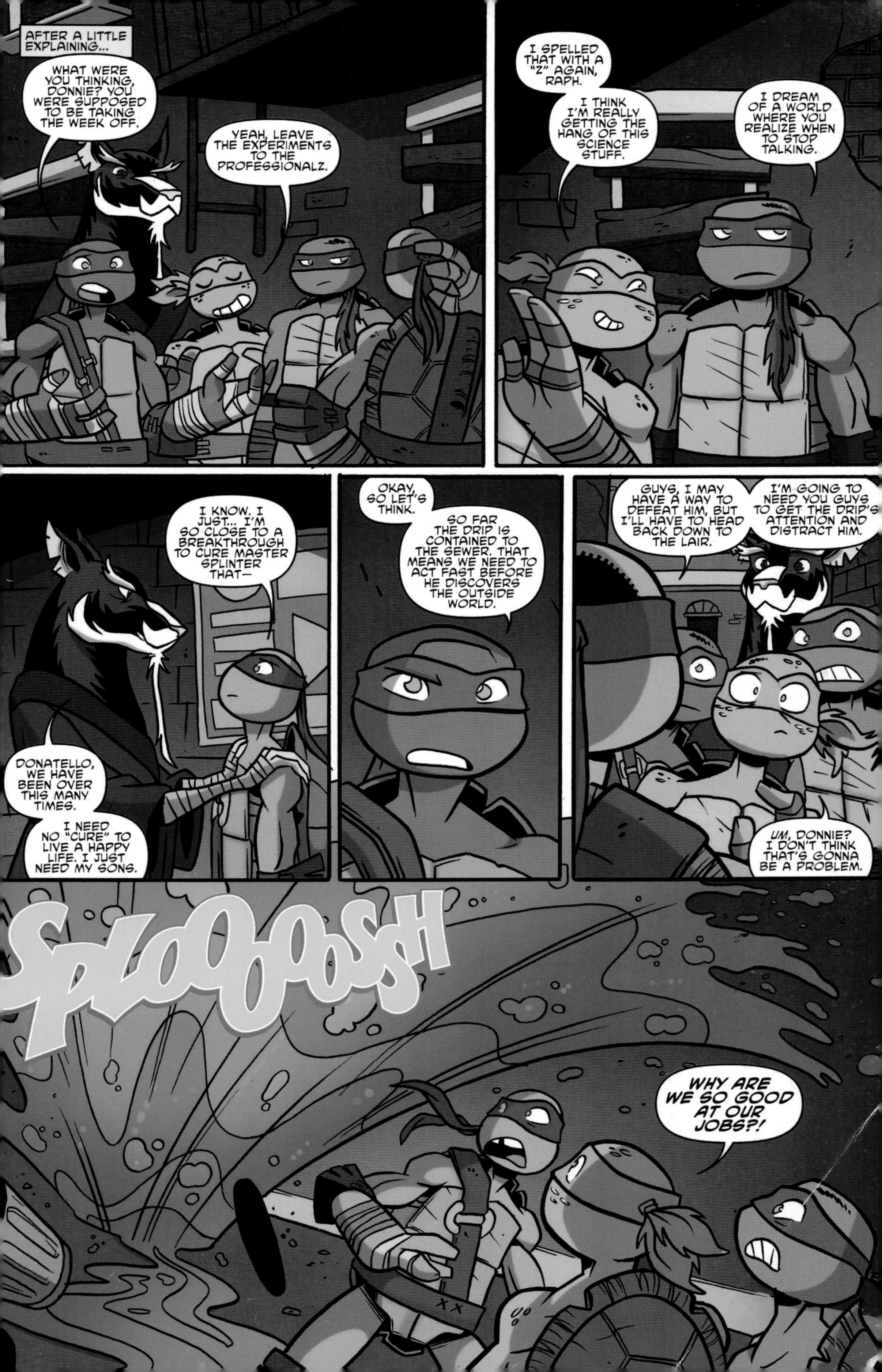
AFTER A LITTLE EXPLAINING...
WHAT WERE YOU THINKING, DONNIE? YOU WERE SUPPOSED TO BE TAKING THE WEEK OFF.
YEAH, LEAVE THE EXPERIMENTS TO THE PROFESSIONALZ.
I SPELLED THAT WITH A "Z" AGAIN, RAPH.
I THINK I'M REALLY GETTING THE HANG OF THIS SCIENCE STUFF.
I DREAM OF A WORLD WHERE YOU REALIZE WHEN TO STOP TALKING.
I KNOW. I JUST... I'M SO CLOSE TO A BREAKTHROUGH TO CURE MASTER SPLINTER THAT—
DONATELLO, WE HAVE BEEN OVER THIS MANY TIMES.
I NEED NO "CURE" TO LIVE A HAPPY LIFE. I JUST NEED MY SONS.
OKAY, SO LET'S THINK.
SO FAR THE DRIP IS CONTAINED TO THE SEWER. THAT MEANS WE NEED TO ACT FAST BEFORE HE DISCOVERS THE OUTSIDE WORLD.
GUYS, I MAY HAVE A WAY TO DEFEAT HIM, BUT I'LL HAVE TO HEAD BACK DOWN TO THE LAIR.
I'M GOING TO NEED YOU GUYS TO GET THE DRIP'S ATTENTION AND DISTRACT HIM.
UM, DONNIE? I DON'T THINK THAT'S GONNA BE A PROBLEM.
SPLOOOOOSH
WHY ARE WE SO GOOD AT OUR JOBS?!

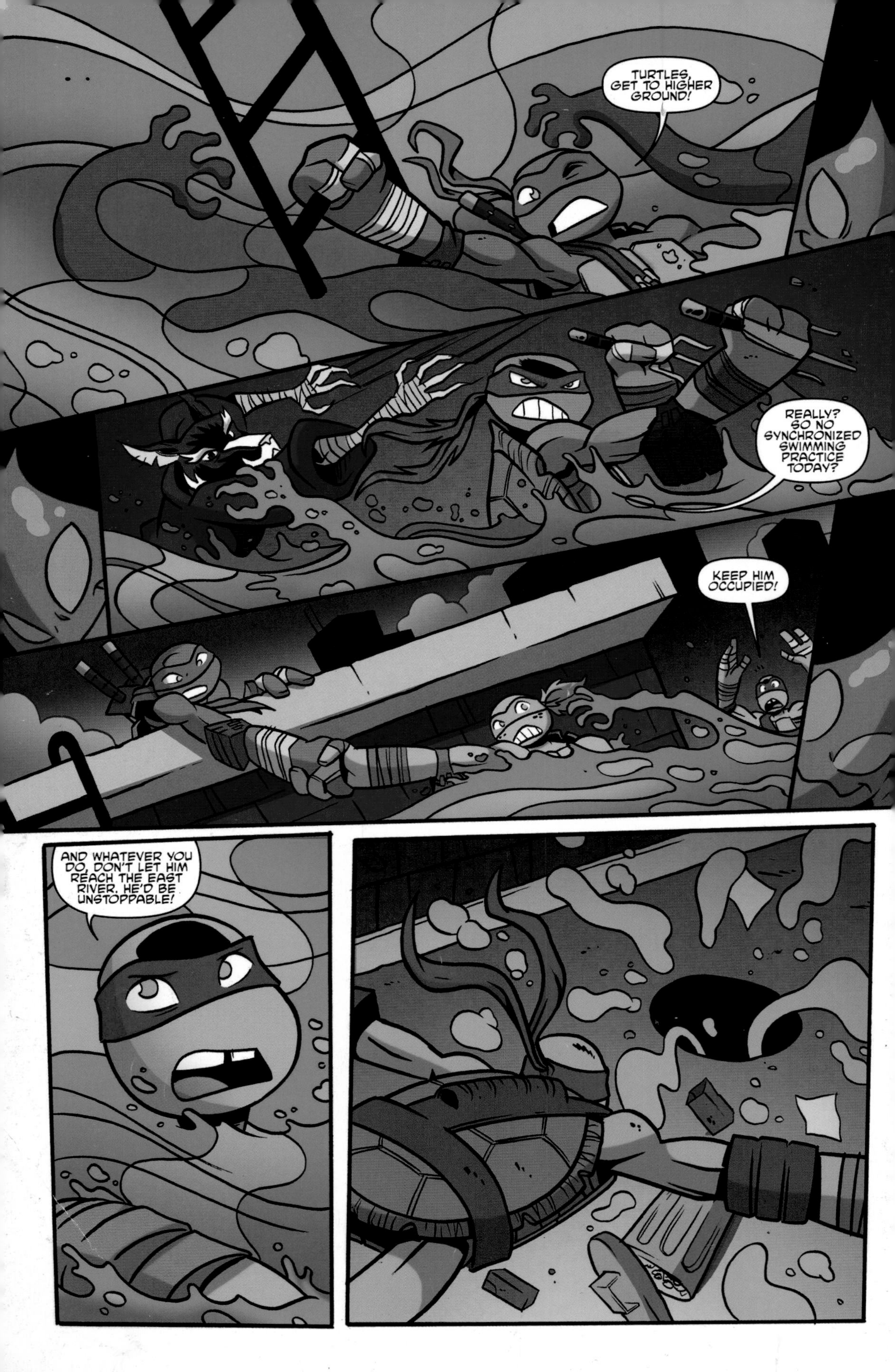
TURTLES, GET TO HIGHER GROUND!
REALLY? SO NO SYNCHRONIZED SWIMMING PRACTICE TODAY?
KEEP HIM OCCUPIED!
AND WHATEVER YOU DO, DON'T LET HIM REACH THE EAST RIVER. HE'D BE UNSTOPPABLE!

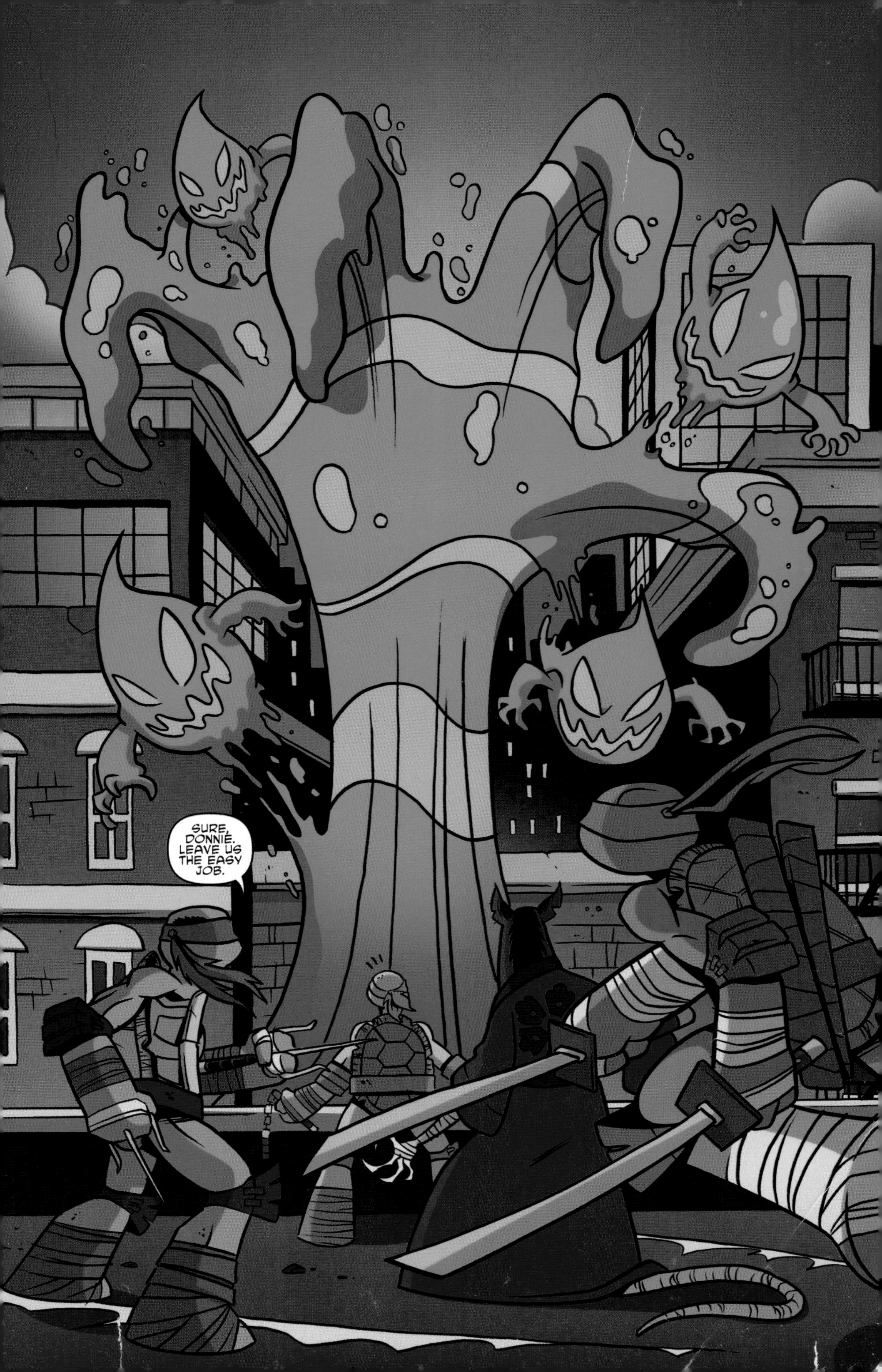
SURE, DONNIE. LEAVE US THE EASY JOB.

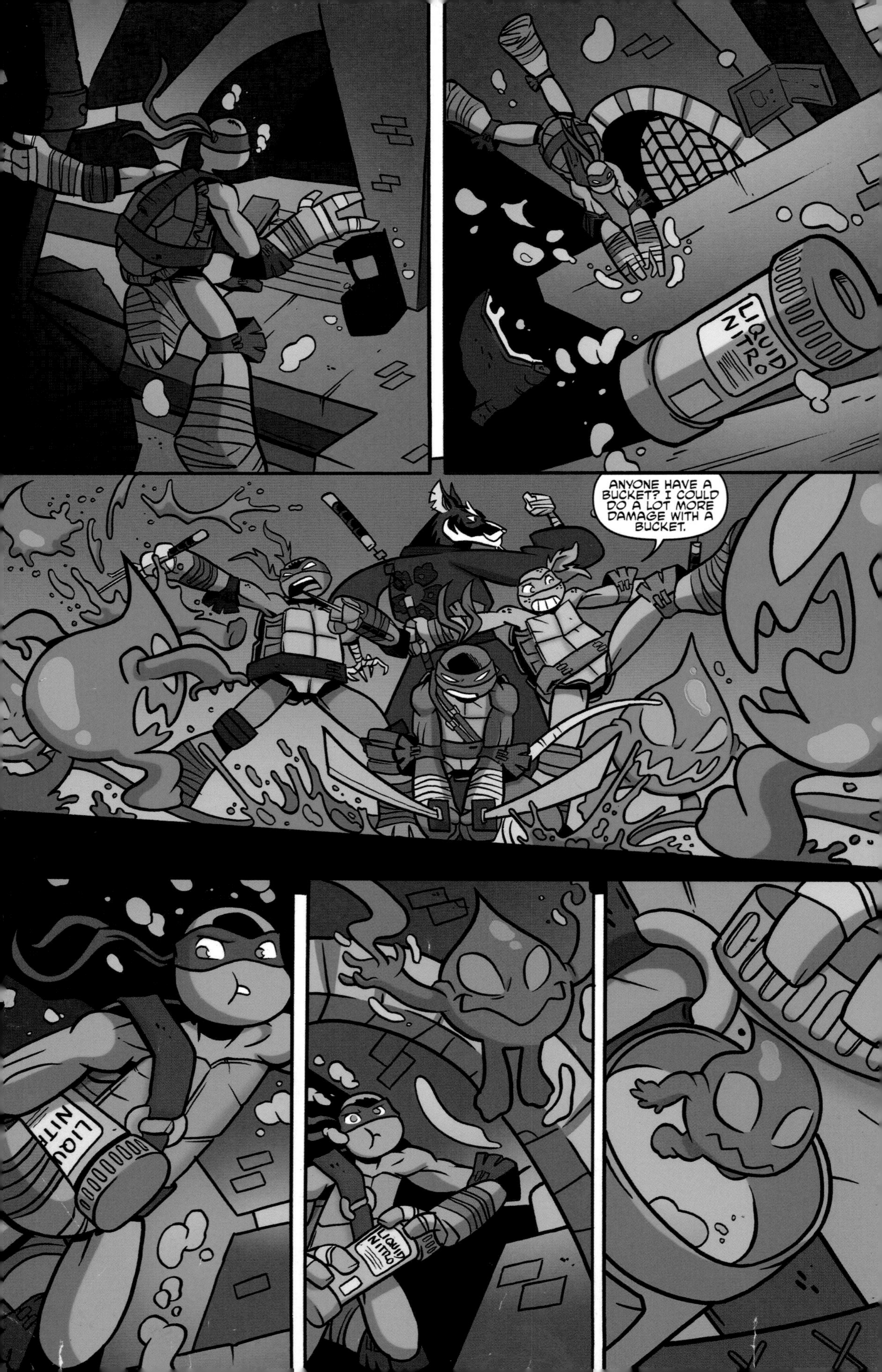
LIQUID NITRO
ANYONE HAVE A BUCKET? I COULD DO A LOT MORE DAMAGE WITH A BUCKET.
LIQU NITR
LIQUID NITRO

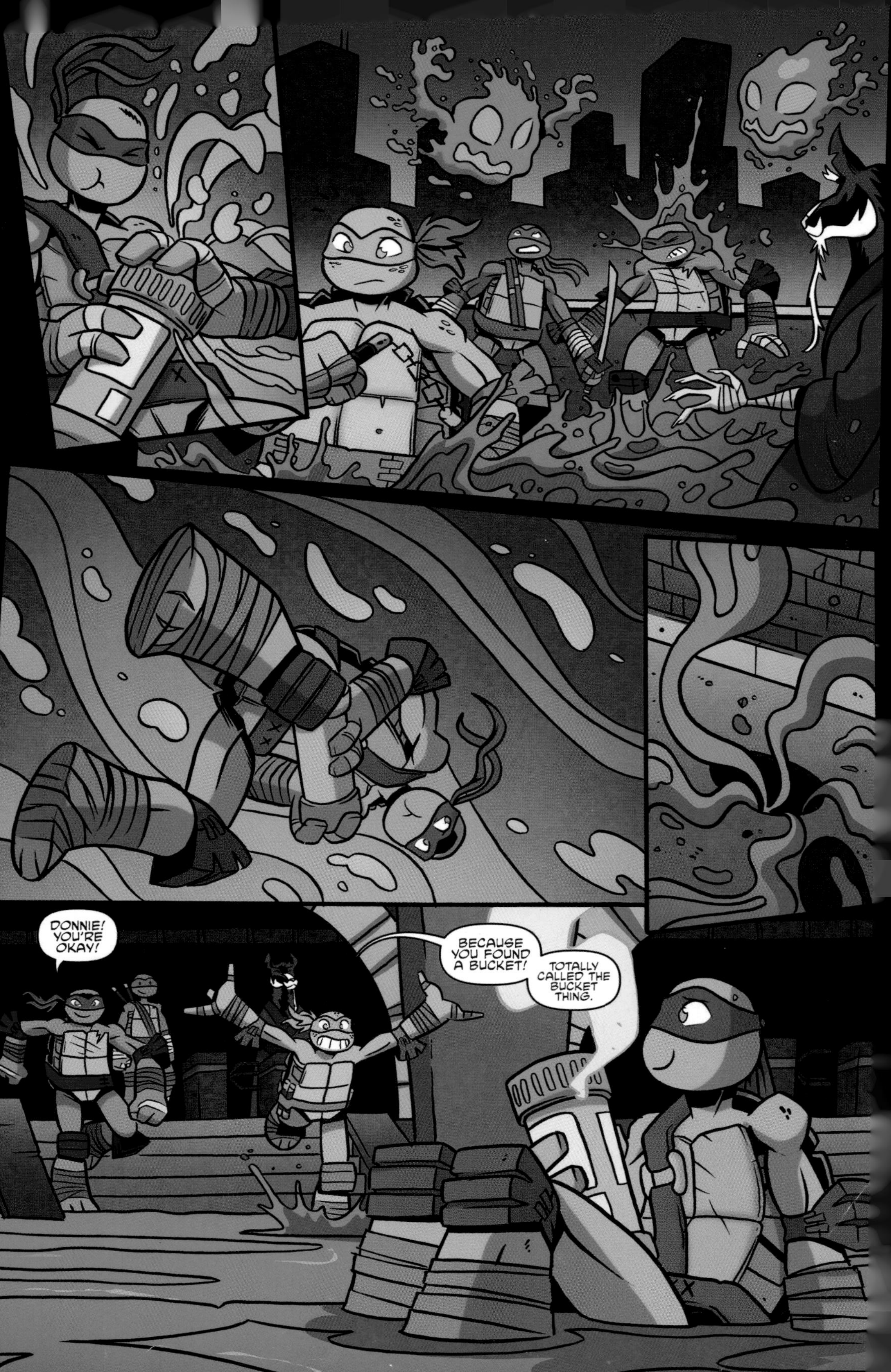
DONNIE! YOU'RE OKAY!
BECAUSE YOU FOUND A BUCKET!
TOTALLY CALLED THE BUCKET THING.

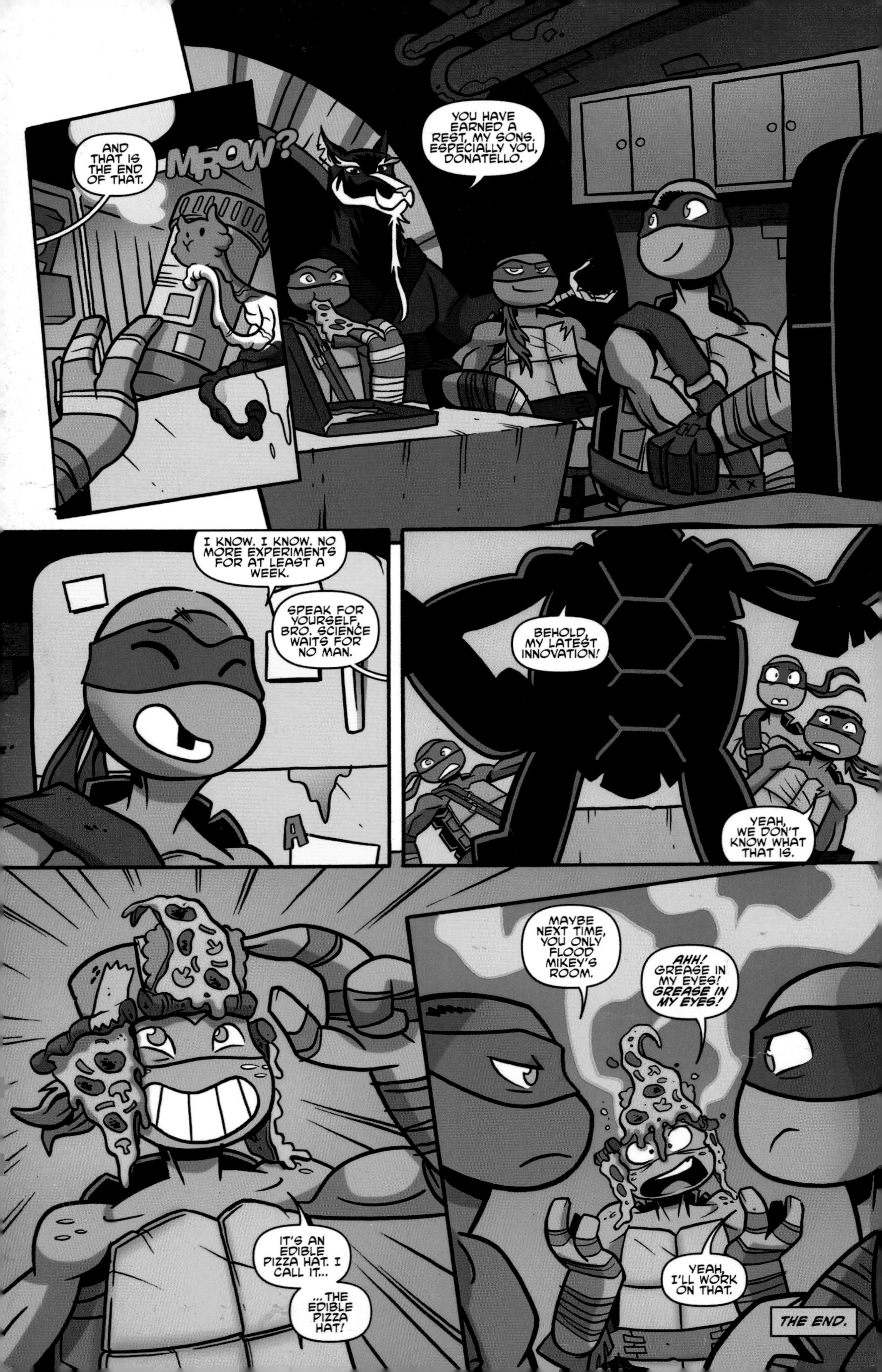
AND THAT IS THE END OF THAT.
MROW?
YOU HAVE EARNED A REST, MY SONS. ESPECIALLY YOU, DONATELLO.
I KNOW. I KNOW. NO MORE EXPERIMENTS FOR AT LEAST A WEEK.
SPEAK FOR YOURSELF, BRO. SCIENCE WAITS FOR NO MAN.
BEHOLD, MY LATEST INNOVATION!
YEAH, WE DON'T KNOW WHAT THAT IS.
IT'S AN EDIBLE PIZZA HAT. I CALL IT...
...THE EDIBLE PIZZA HAT!
MAYBE NEXT TIME, YOU ONLY FLOOD MIKEY'S ROOM.
AHH! GREASE IN MY EYES! GREASE IN MY EYES!
YEAH, I'LL WORK ON THAT.
THE END.

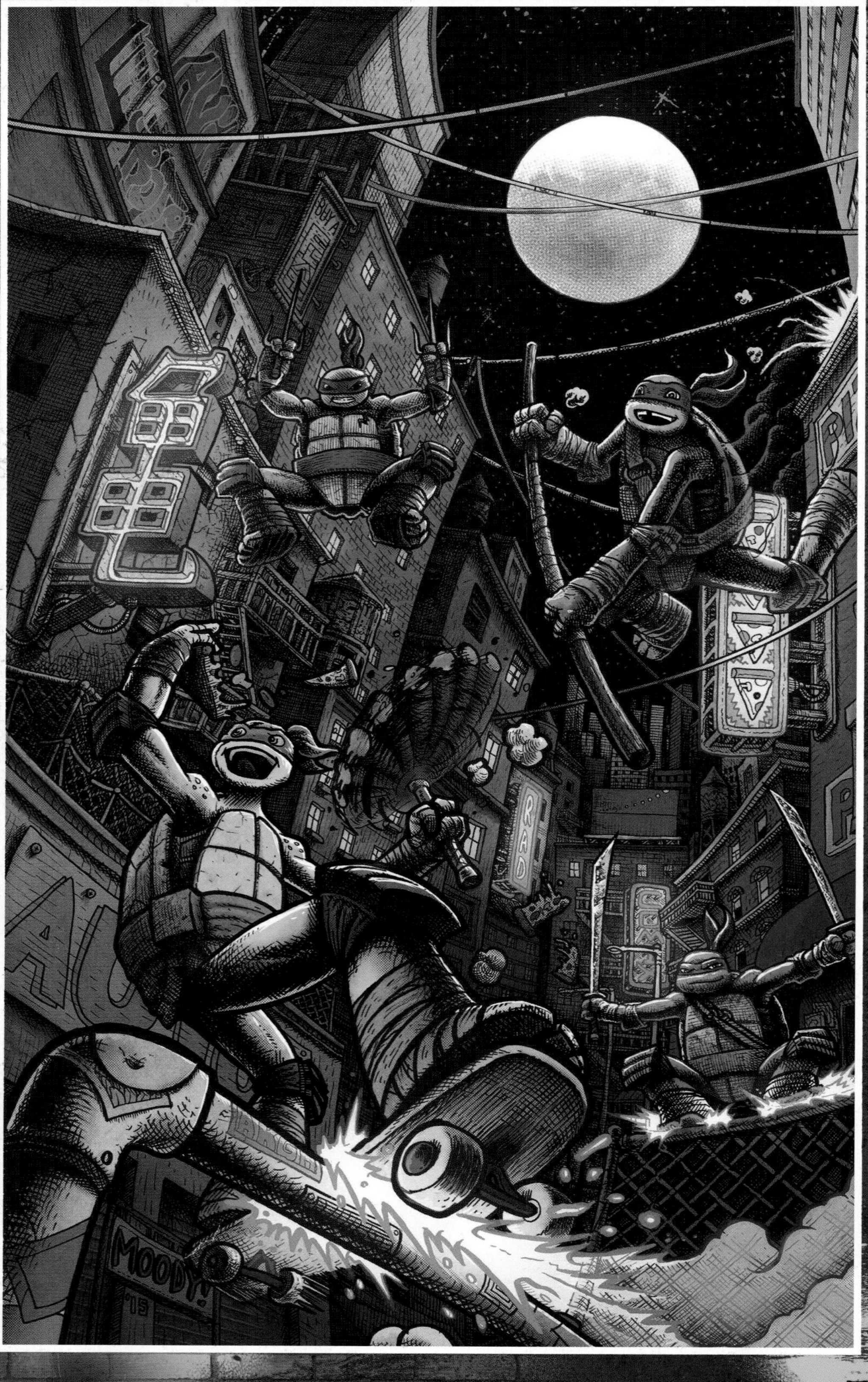
RAD
MOODY!
'13

ART BY BUSTER MOODY

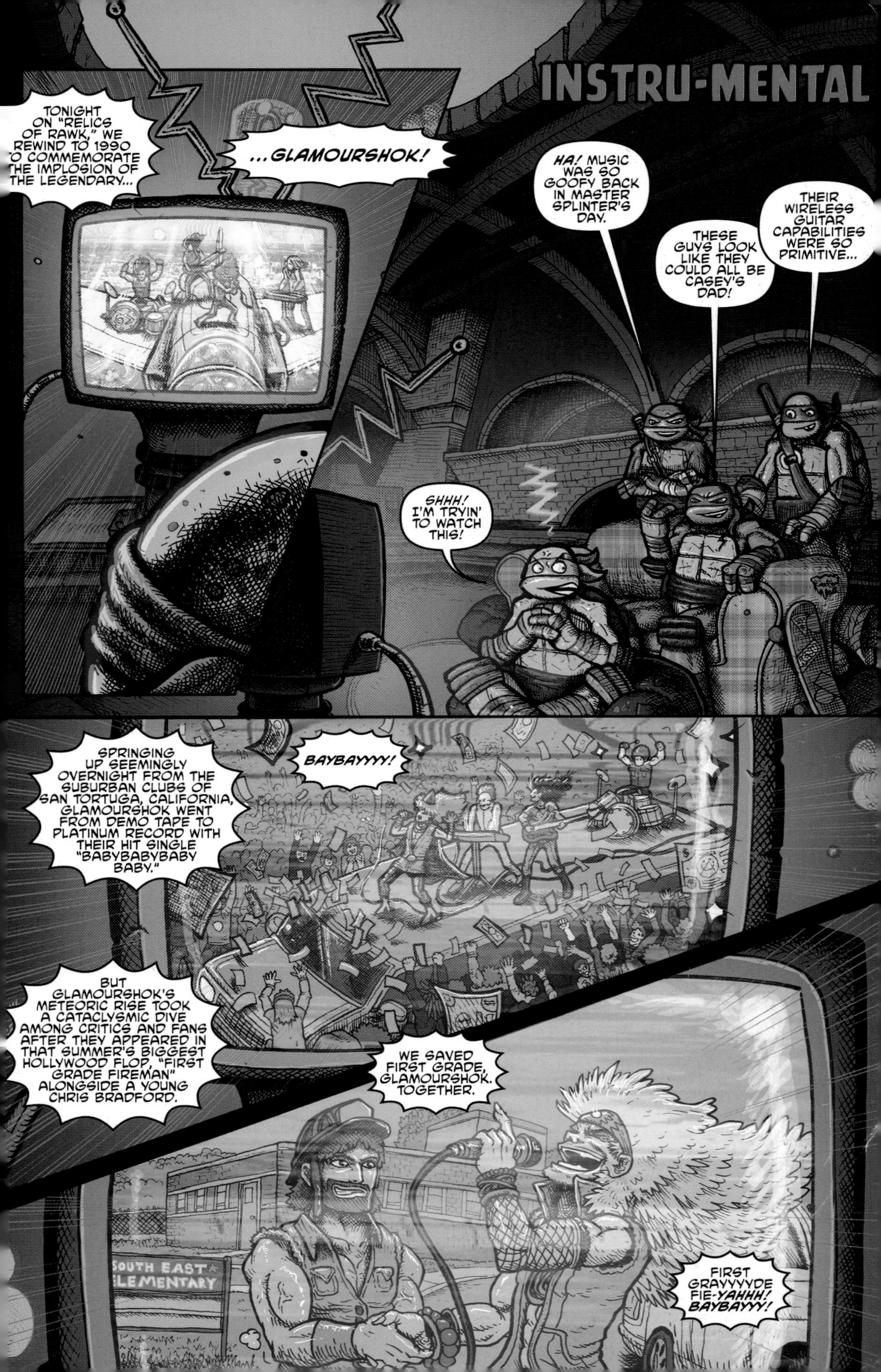
INSTRU-MENTAL
TONIGHT ON "RELICS OF RAWK," WE REWIND TO 1990 TO COMMEMORATE THE IMPLOSION OF THE LEGENDARY...
...GLAMOURSHOK!
HA! MUSIC WAS SO GOOFY BACK IN MASTER SPLINTER'S DAY.
THESE GUYS LOOK LIKE THEY COULD ALL BE CASEY'S DAD!
THEIR WIRELESS GUITAR CAPABILITIES WERE SO PRIMITIVE...
SHHH! I'M TRYIN' TO WATCH THIS!
SPRINGING UP SEEMINGLY OVERNIGHT FROM THE SUBURBAN CLUBS OF SAN TORTUGA, CALIFORNIA, GLAMOURSHOK WENT FROM DEMO TAPE TO PLATINUM RECORD WITH THEIR HIT SINGLE "BABYBABYBABY BABY."
BAYBAYYYY!
BUT GLAMOURSHOK'S METEORIC RISE TOOK A CATACLYSMIC DIVE AMONG CRITICS AND FANS AFTER THEY APPEARED IN THAT SUMMER'S BIGGEST HOLLYWOOD FLOP, "FIRST GRADE FIREMAN" ALONGSIDE A YOUNG CHRIS BRADFORD.
WE SAVED FIRST GRADE, GLAMOURSHOK. TOGETHER.
SOUTH EAST ELEMENTARY
FIRST GRAYYYYDE FIE-YAHHH! BAYBAYYY!

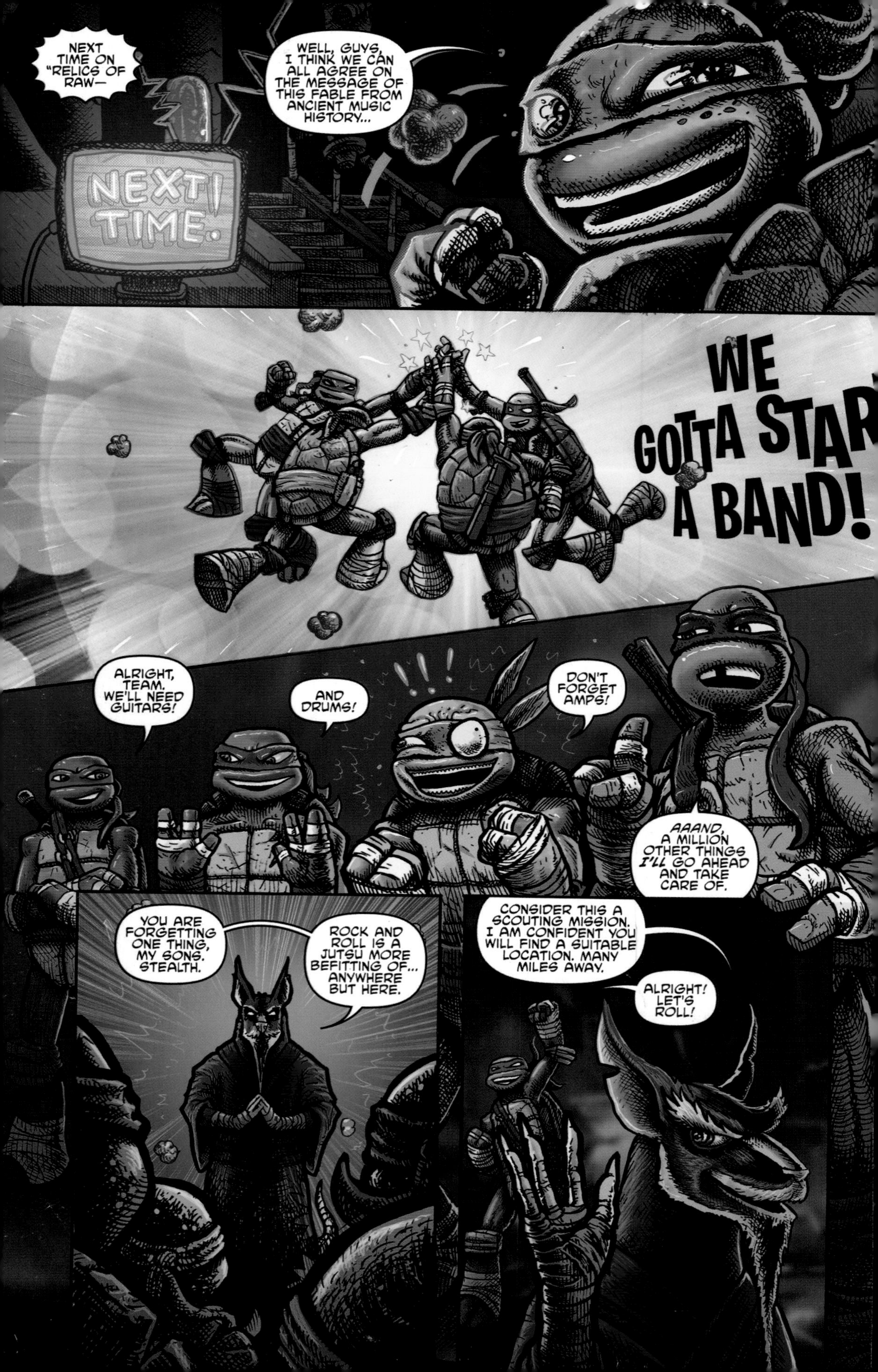
NEXT TIME ON "RELICS OF RAW—
NEXT TIME.
WELL, GUYS, I THINK WE CAN ALL AGREE ON THE MESSAGE OF THIS FABLE FROM ANCIENT MUSIC HISTORY...
WE GOTTA STAR A BAND!
ALRIGHT, TEAM. WE'LL NEED GUITARS!
AND DRUMS!
DON'T FORGET AMPS!
AAAND, A MILLION OTHER THINGS *I'LL* GO AHEAD AND TAKE CARE OF.
YOU ARE FORGETTING ONE THING, MY SONS. STEALTH.
ROCK AND ROLL IS A JUTSU MORE BEFITTING OF... ANYWHERE BUT HERE.
CONSIDER THIS A SCOUTING MISSION. I AM CONFIDENT YOU WILL FIND A SUITABLE LOCATION. MANY MILES AWAY.
ALRIGHT! LET'S ROLL!

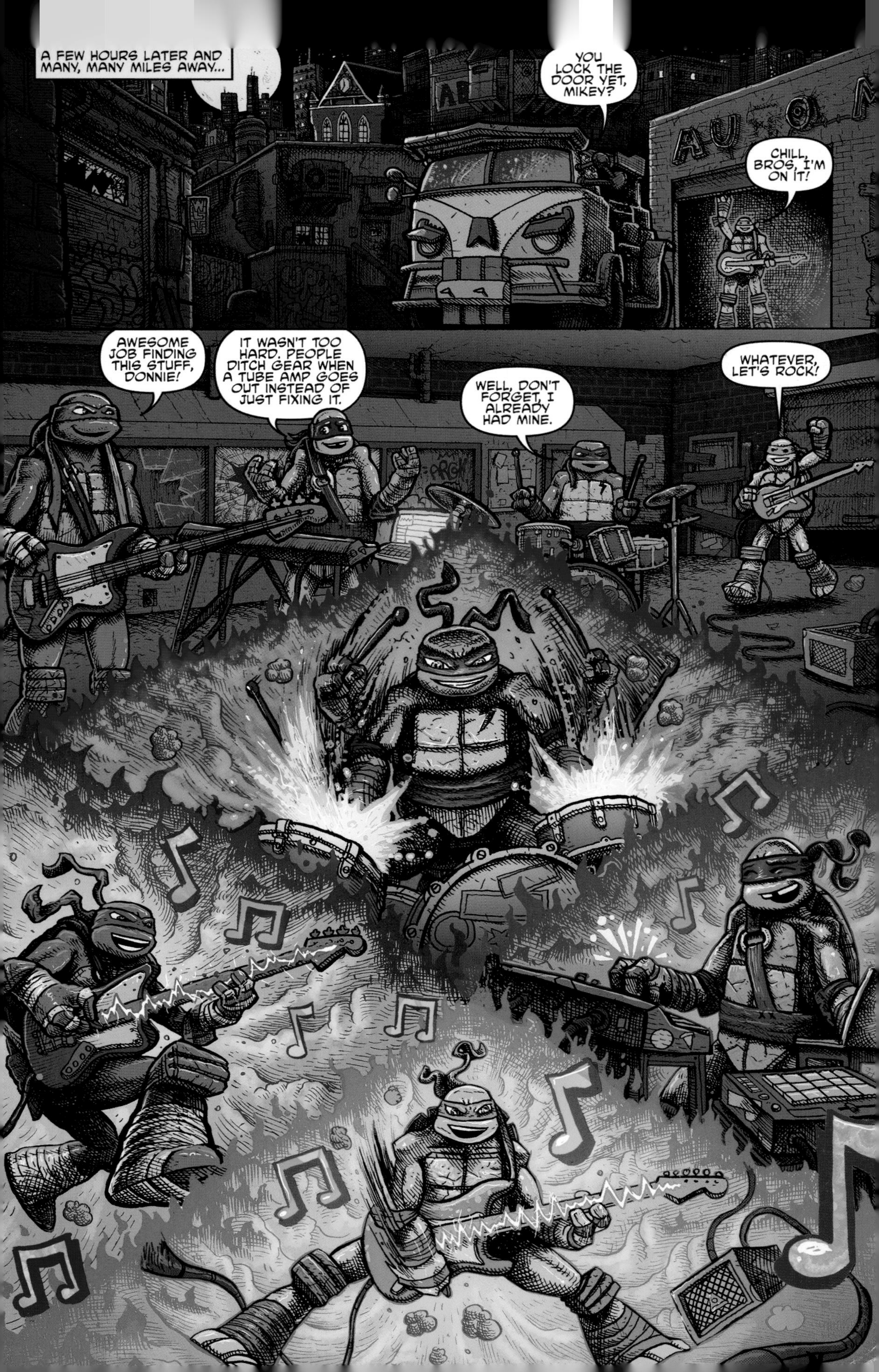
A FEW HOURS LATER AND MANY, MANY MILES AWAY...
YOU LOCK THE DOOR YET, MIKEY?
CHILL, BROS, I'M ON IT!
AWESOME JOB FINDING THIS STUFF, DONNIE!
IT WASN'T TOO HARD. PEOPLE DITCH GEAR WHEN A TUBE AMP GOES OUT INSTEAD OF JUST FIXING IT.
WELL, DON'T FORGET, I ALREADY HAD MINE.
WHATEVER, LET'S ROCK!

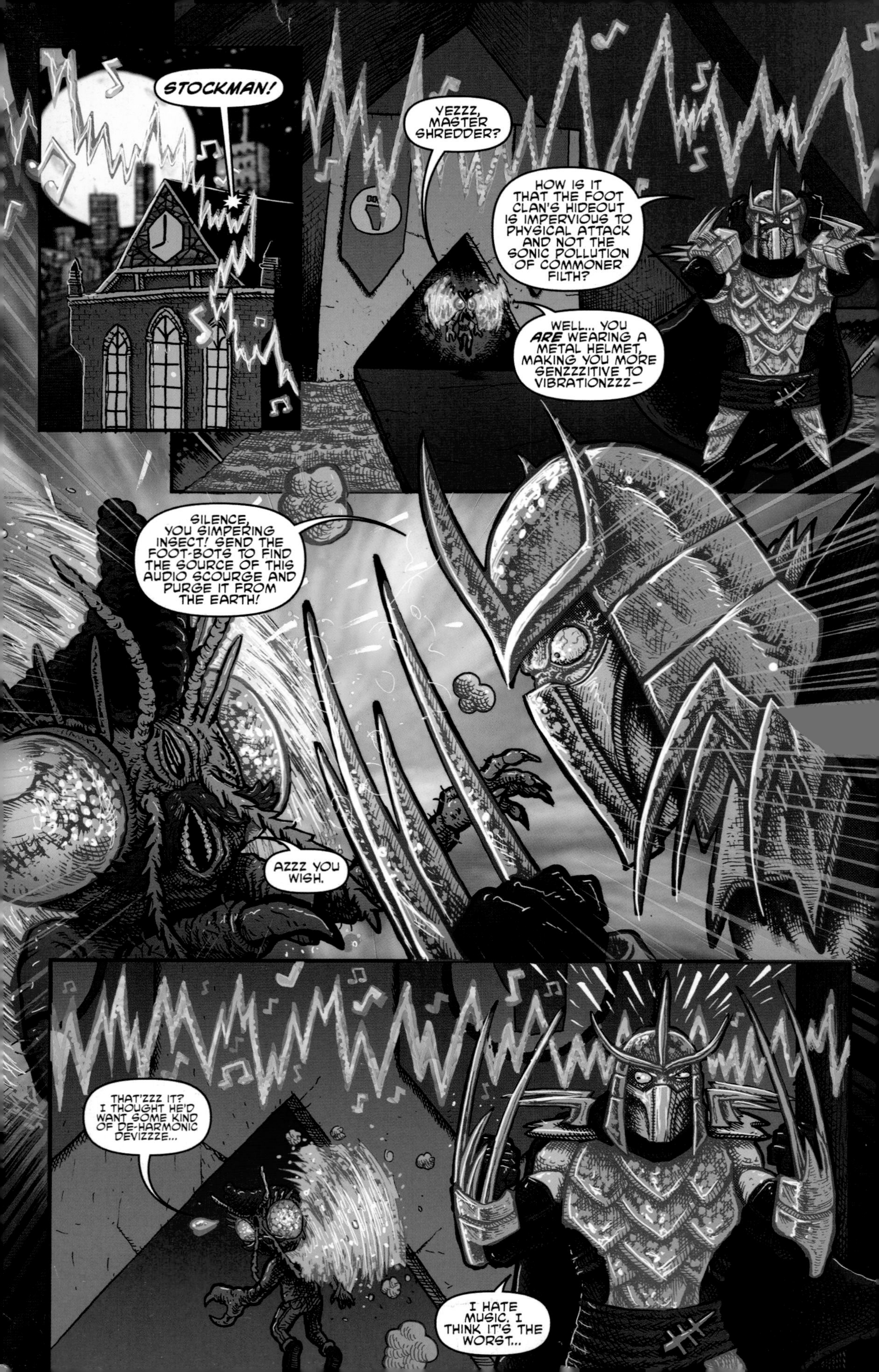
STOCKMAN!
YEZZZ, MASTER SHREDDER?
HOW IS IT THAT THE FOOT CLAN'S HIDEOUT IS IMPERVIOUS TO PHYSICAL ATTACK AND NOT THE SONIC POLLUTION OF COMMONER FILTH?
WELL... YOU *ARE* WEARING A METAL HELMET, MAKING YOU MORE SENZZZITIVE TO VIBRATIONZZZ—
SILENCE, YOU SIMPERING INSECT! SEND THE FOOT-BOTS TO FIND THE SOURCE OF THIS AUDIO SCOURGE AND PURGE IT FROM THE EARTH!
AZZZ YOU WISH.
THAT'ZZZ IT? I THOUGHT HE'D WANT SOME KIND OF DE-HARMONIC DEVIZZZE...
I HATE MUSIC. I THINK IT'S THE WORST...

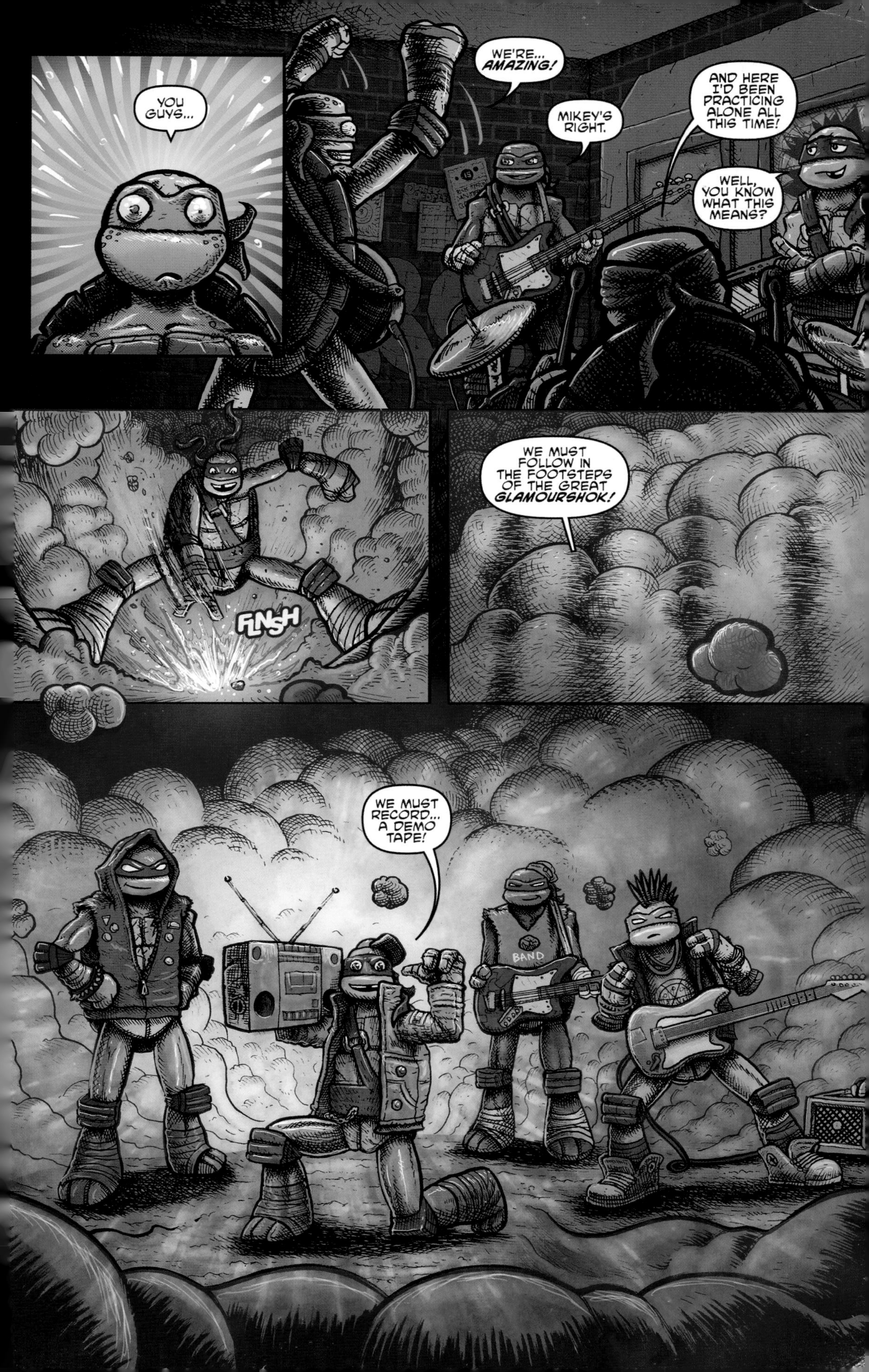
YOU GUYS...
WE'RE... AMAZING!
MIKEY'S RIGHT.
AND HERE I'D BEEN PRACTICING ALONE ALL THIS TIME!
WELL, YOU KNOW WHAT THIS MEANS?
FLNSH
WE MUST FOLLOW IN THE FOOTSTEPS OF THE GREAT GLAMOURSHOK!
WE MUST RECORD... A DEMO TAPE!
BAND

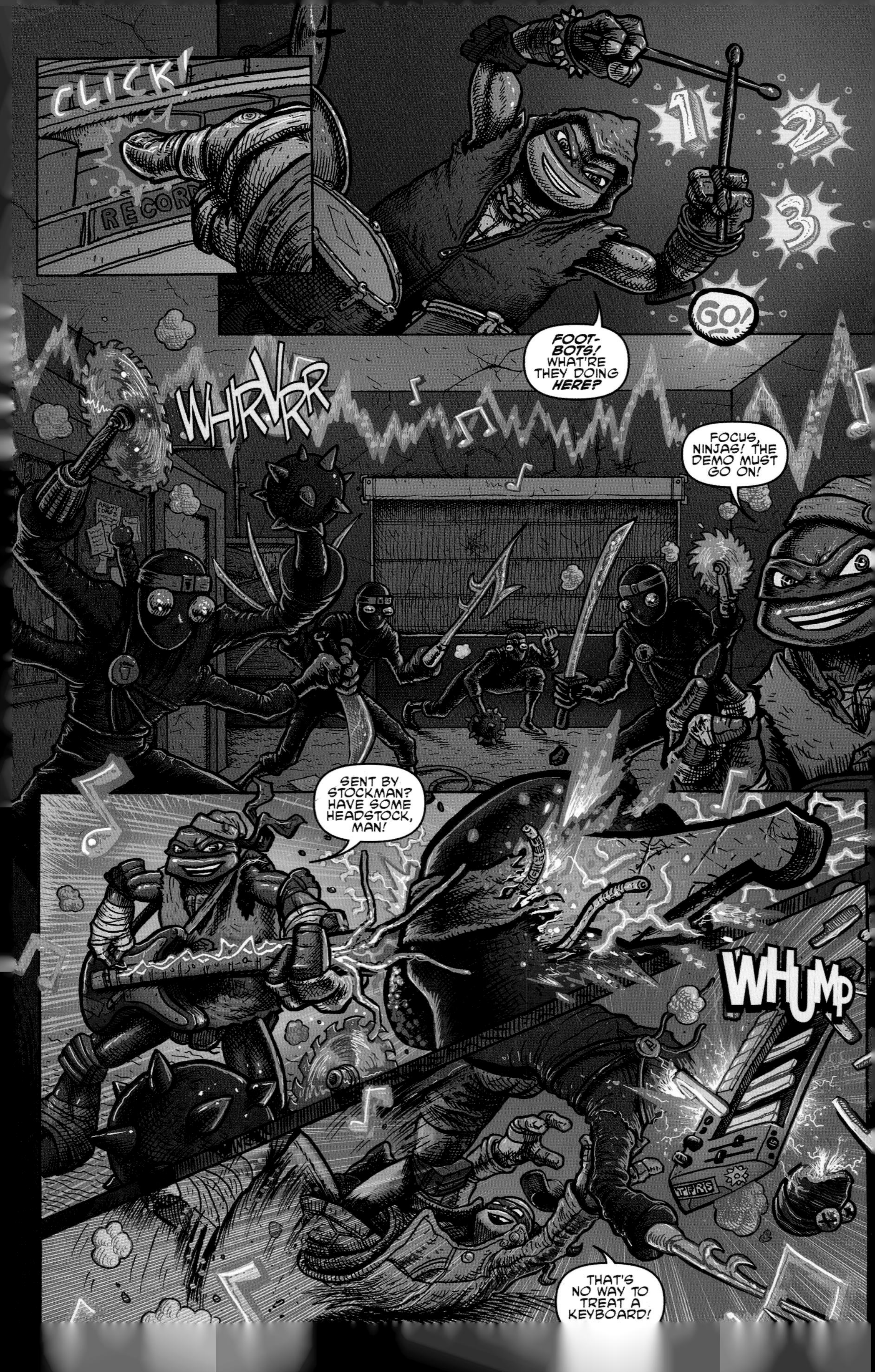

CLICK!
RECORD
1
2
3
GO!
FOOT-BOTS! WHAT'RE THEY DOING HERE?
WHRVRR
FOCUS, NINJAS! THE DEMO MUST GO ON!
SENT BY STOCKMAN? HAVE SOME HEADSTOCK, MAN!
WHUMP
THAT'S NO WAY TO TREAT A KEYBOARD!

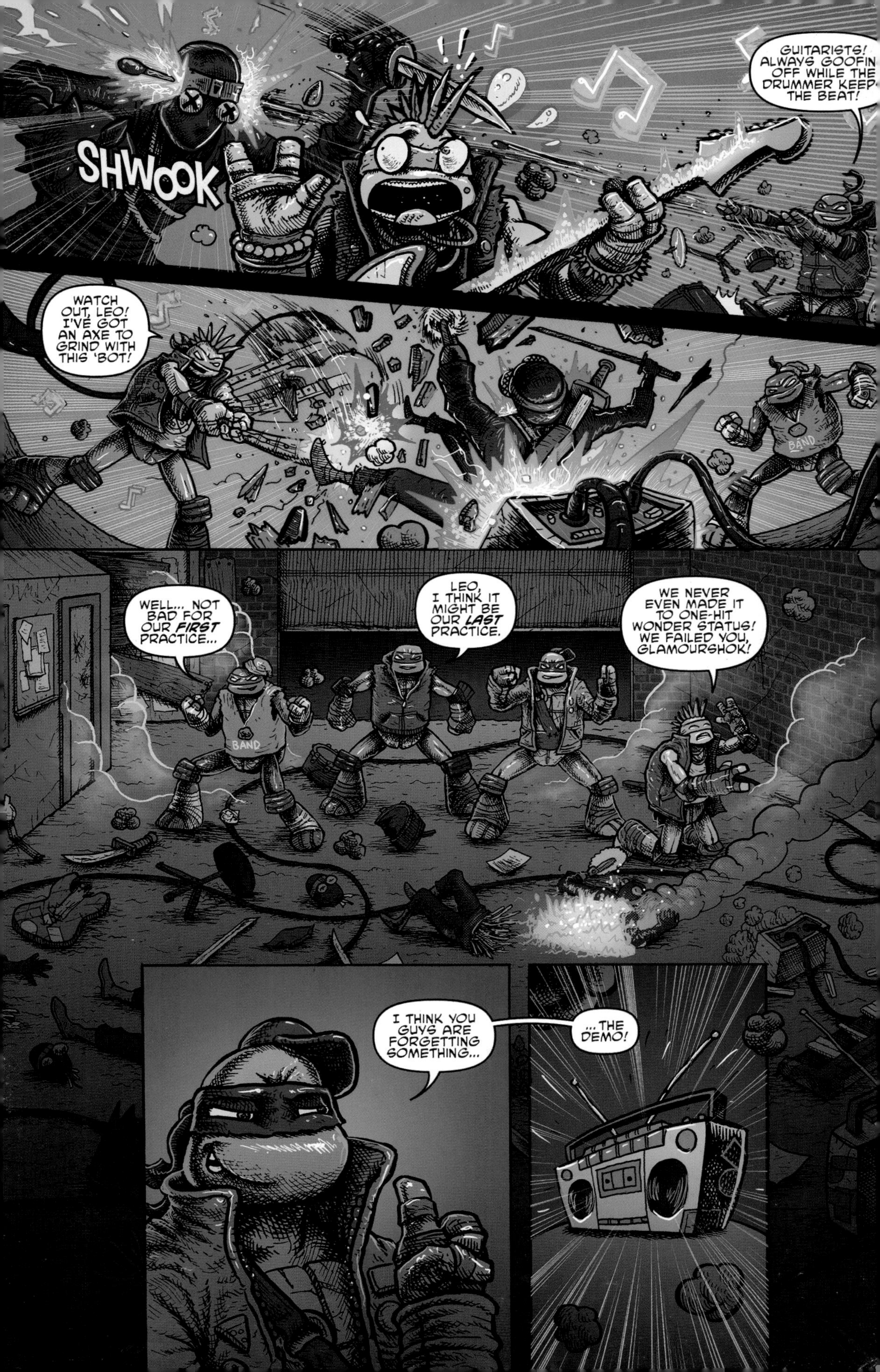
SHWOOK
GUITARISTS! ALWAYS GOOFIN OFF WHILE THE DRUMMER KEEP THE BEAT!
WATCH OUT, LEO! I'VE GOT AN AXE TO GRIND WITH THIS 'BOT!
BAND
WELL... NOT BAD FOR OUR *FIRST* PRACTICE...
LEO, I THINK IT MIGHT BE OUR *LAST* PRACTICE.
WE NEVER EVEN MADE IT TO ONE-HIT WONDER STATUS! WE FAILED YOU, GLAMOURSHOK!
BAND
I THINK YOU GUYS ARE FORGETTING SOMETHING...
...THE DEMO!

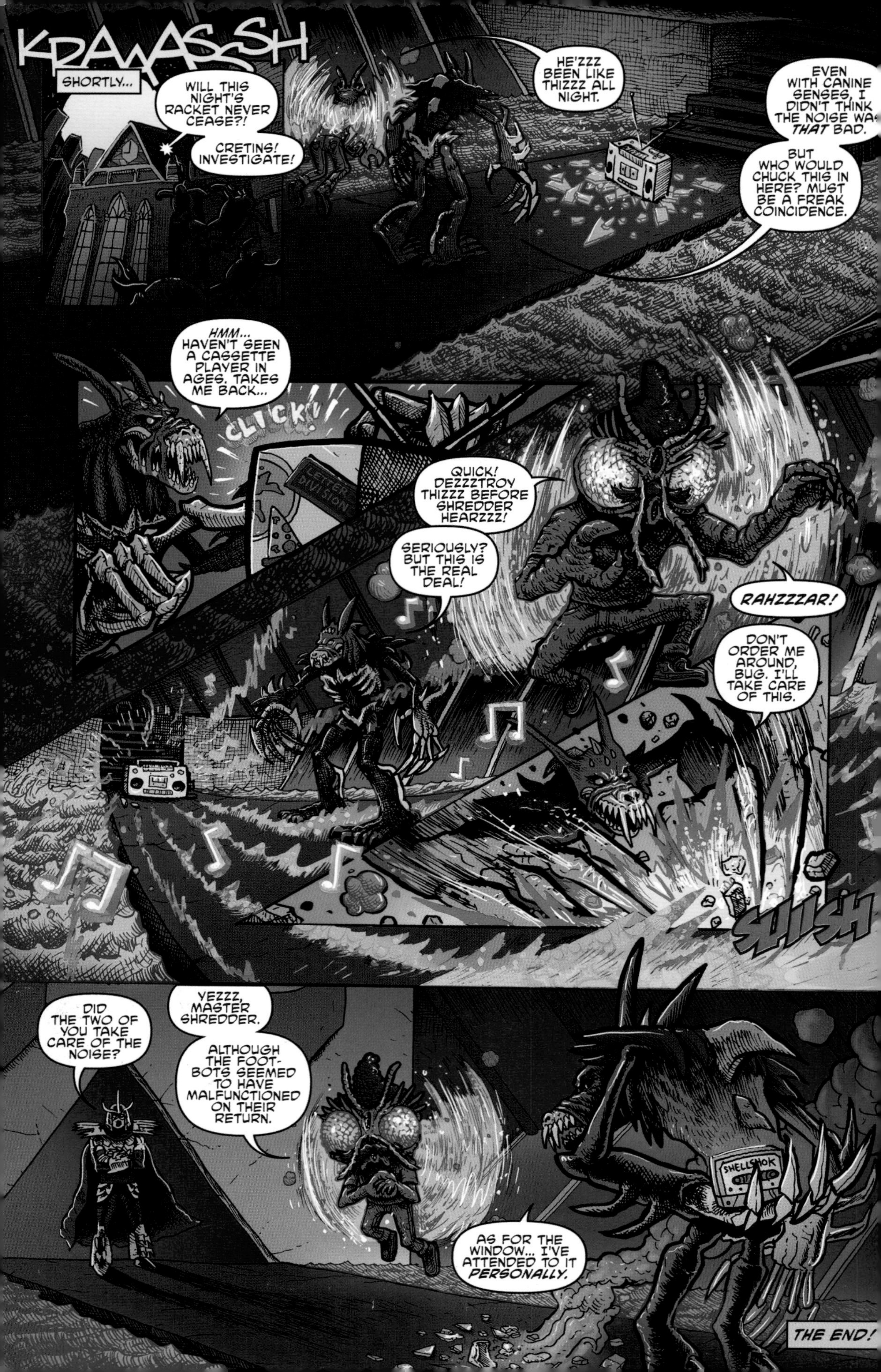
KRAWASSH
SHORTLY...
WILL THIS NIGHT'S RACKET NEVER CEASE?!
CRETINS! INVESTIGATE!
HE'ZZZ BEEN LIKE THIZZZ ALL NIGHT.
EVEN WITH CANINE SENSES, I DIDN'T THINK THE NOISE WAS THAT BAD.
BUT WHO WOULD CHUCK THIS IN HERE? MUST BE A FREAK COINCIDENCE.
HMM... HAVEN'T SEEN A CASSETTE PLAYER IN AGES. TAKES ME BACK...
CLICK!
LETTER DIVISION
QUICK! DEZZZTROY THIZZZ BEFORE SHREDDER HEARZZZ!
SERIOUSLY? BUT THIS IS THE REAL DEAL!
RAHZZZAR!
DON'T ORDER ME AROUND, BUG. I'LL TAKE CARE OF THIS.
SHHSH
DID THE TWO OF YOU TAKE CARE OF THE NOISE?
YEZZZ, MASTER SHREDDER.
ALTHOUGH THE FOOT-BOTS SEEMED TO HAVE MALFUNCTIONED ON THEIR RETURN.
SHELLSHOK
AS FOR THE WINDOW... I'VE ATTENDED TO IT PERSONALLY.
THE END!

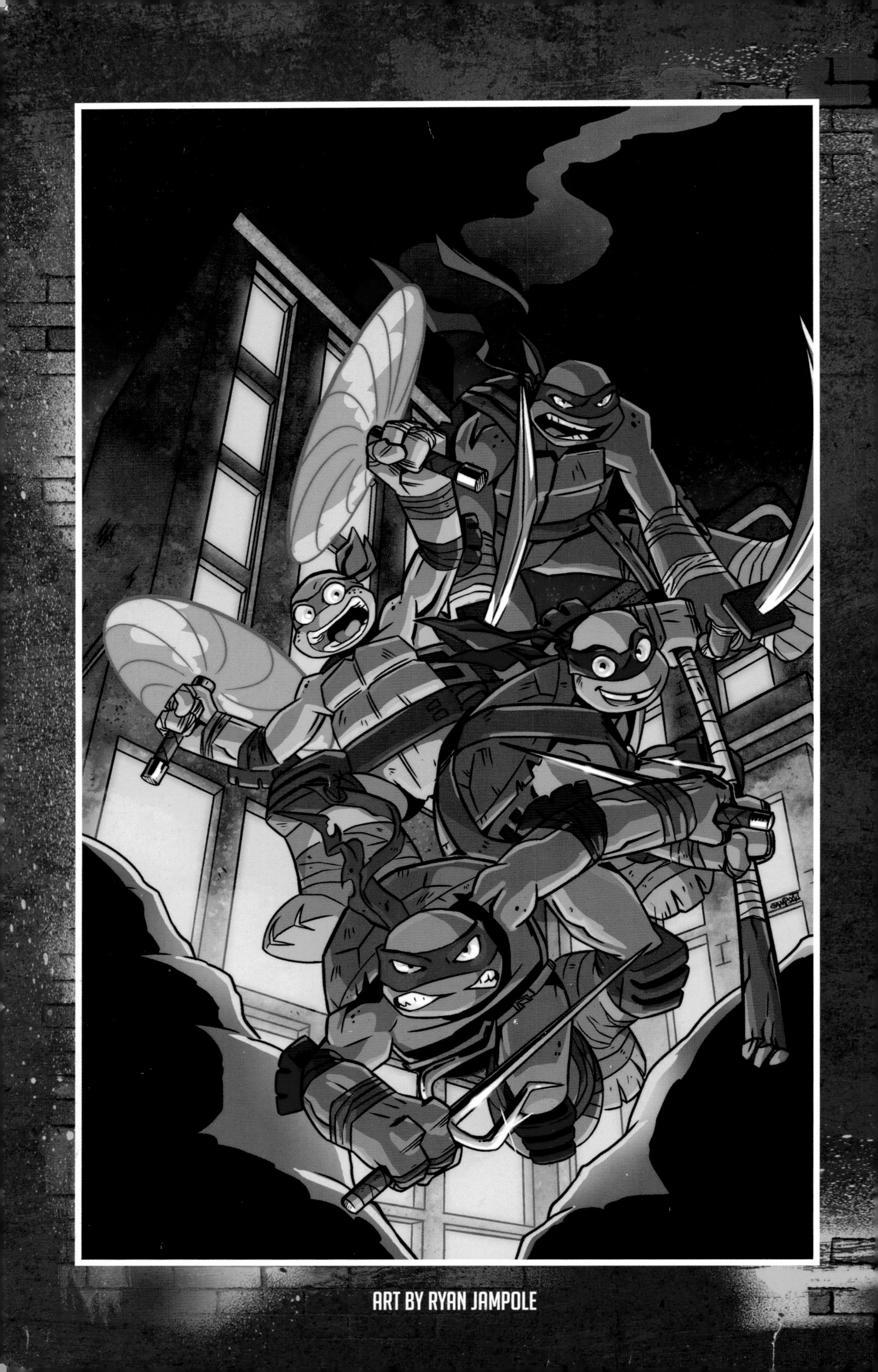

ART BY RYAN JAMPOLE

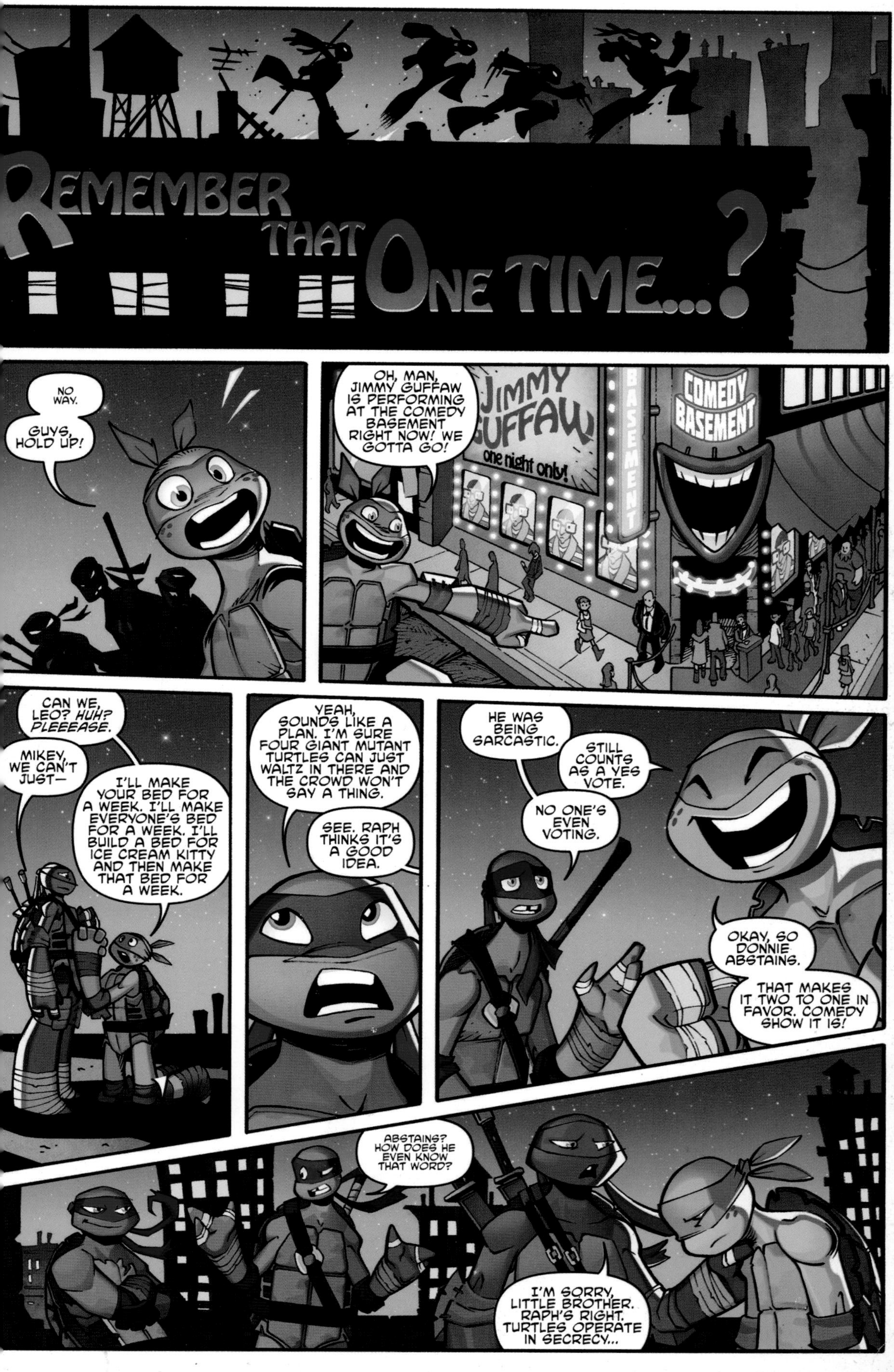
REMEMBER THAT ONE TIME...?
NO WAY.
GUYS, HOLD UP!
OH, MAN, JIMMY GUFFAW IS PERFORMING AT THE COMEDY BASEMENT RIGHT NOW! WE GOTTA GO!
JIMMY GUFFAW
one night only!
BASEMENT
COMEDY BASEMENT
CAN WE, LEO? HUH? PLEEEASE.
MIKEY, WE CAN'T JUST—
I'LL MAKE YOUR BED FOR A WEEK. I'LL MAKE EVERYONE'S BED FOR A WEEK. I'LL BUILD A BED FOR ICE CREAM KITTY AND THEN MAKE THAT BED FOR A WEEK.
YEAH, SOUNDS LIKE A PLAN. I'M SURE FOUR GIANT MUTANT TURTLES CAN JUST WALTZ IN THERE AND THE CROWD WON'T SAY A THING.
SEE. RAPH THINKS IT'S A GOOD IDEA.
HE WAS BEING SARCASTIC.
STILL COUNTS AS A YES VOTE.
NO ONE'S EVEN VOTING.
OKAY, SO DONNIE ABSTAINS.
THAT MAKES IT TWO TO ONE IN FAVOR. COMEDY SHOW IT IS!
ABSTAINS? HOW DOES HE EVEN KNOW THAT WORD?
I'M SORRY, LITTLE BROTHER. RAPH'S RIGHT. TURTLES OPERATE IN SECRECY...

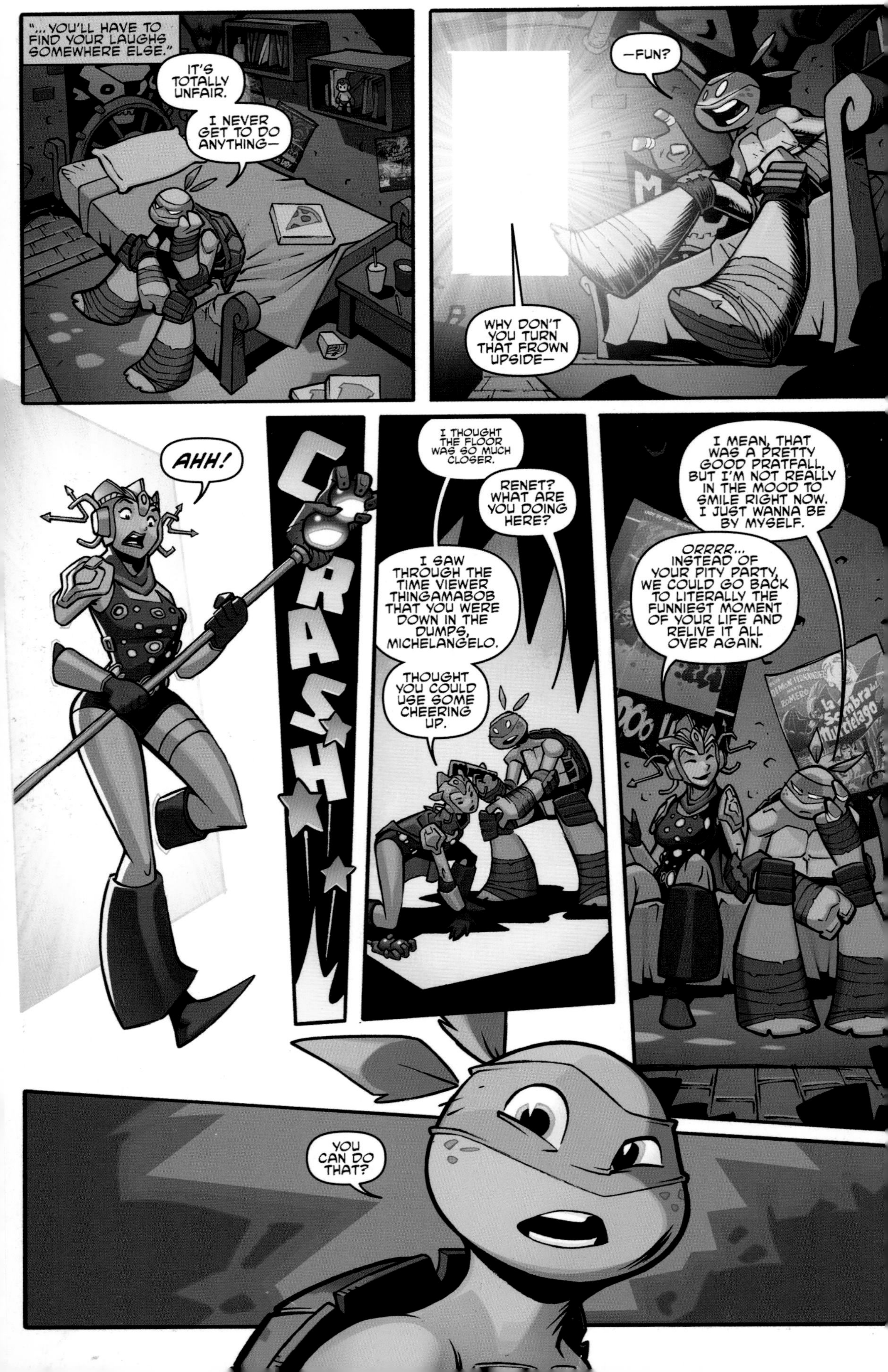
"...YOU'LL HAVE TO FIND YOUR LAUGHS SOMEWHERE ELSE."
IT'S TOTALLY UNFAIR.
I NEVER GET TO DO ANYTHING—
—FUN?
WHY DON'T YOU TURN THAT FROWN UPSIDE—
AHH!
CRASH
I THOUGHT THE FLOOR WAS SO MUCH CLOSER.
RENET? WHAT ARE YOU DOING HERE?
I SAW THROUGH THE TIME VIEWER THINGAMABOB THAT YOU WERE DOWN IN THE DUMPS, MICHELANGELO.
THOUGHT YOU COULD USE SOME CHEERING UP.
I MEAN, THAT WAS A PRETTY GOOD PRATFALL, BUT I'M NOT REALLY IN THE MOOD TO SMILE RIGHT NOW. I JUST WANNA BE BY MYSELF.
ORRRR... INSTEAD OF YOUR PITY PARTY, WE COULD GO BACK TO LITERALLY THE FUNNIEST MOMENT OF YOUR LIFE AND RELIVE IT ALL OVER AGAIN.
YOU CAN DO THAT?

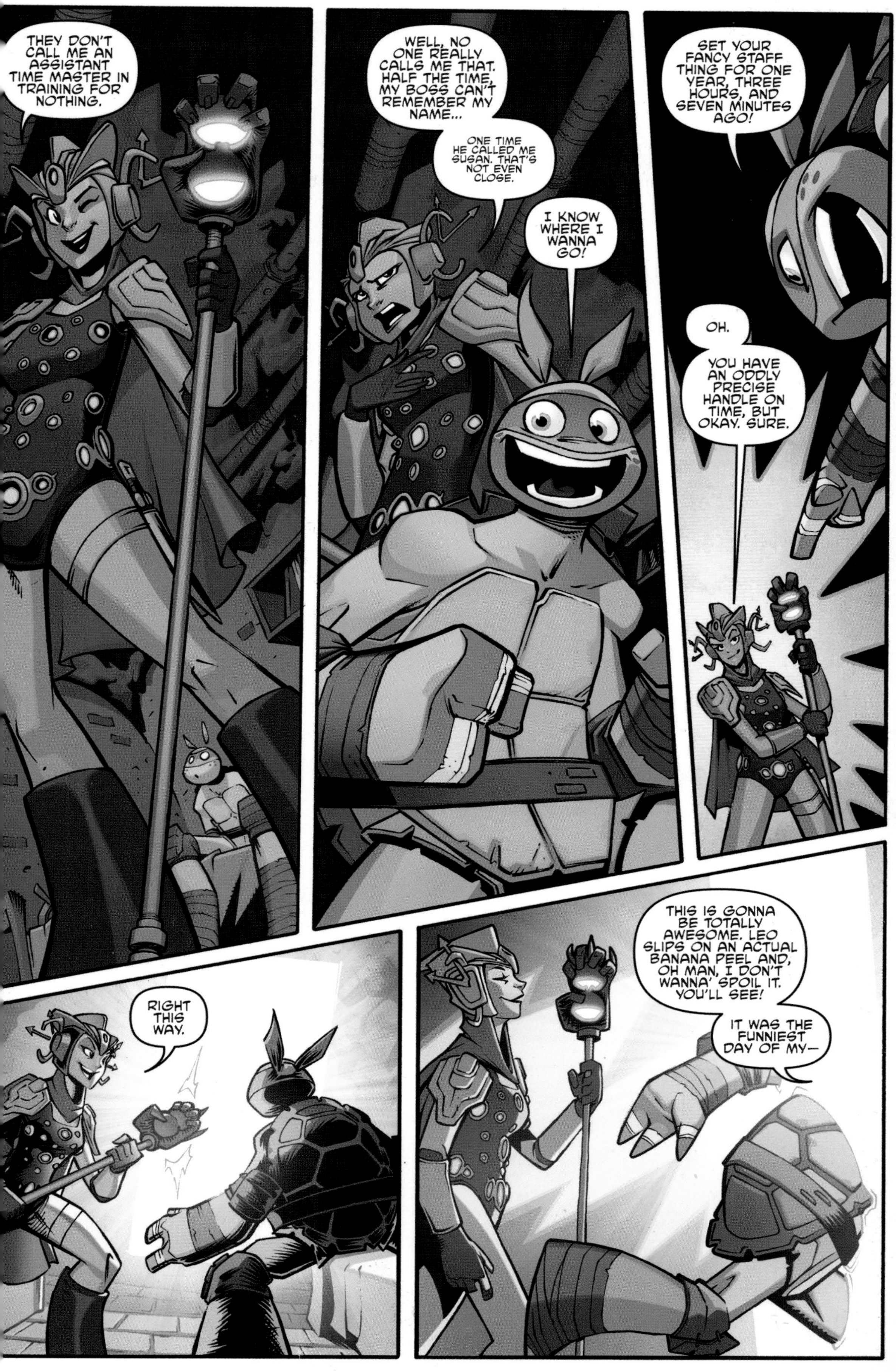
THEY DON'T CALL ME AN ASSISTANT TIME MASTER IN TRAINING FOR NOTHING.
WELL, NO ONE REALLY CALLS ME THAT. HALF THE TIME, MY BOSS CAN'T REMEMBER MY NAME...
ONE TIME HE CALLED ME SUSAN. THAT'S NOT EVEN CLOSE.
I KNOW WHERE I WANNA GO!
SET YOUR FANCY STAFF THING FOR ONE YEAR, THREE HOURS, AND SEVEN MINUTES AGO!
OH.
YOU HAVE AN ODDLY PRECISE HANDLE ON TIME, BUT OKAY. SURE.
RIGHT THIS WAY.
THIS IS GONNA BE TOTALLY AWESOME. LEO SLIPS ON AN ACTUAL BANANA PEEL AND, OH MAN, I DON'T WANNA' SPOIL IT. YOU'LL SEE!
IT WAS THE FUNNIEST DAY OF MY—

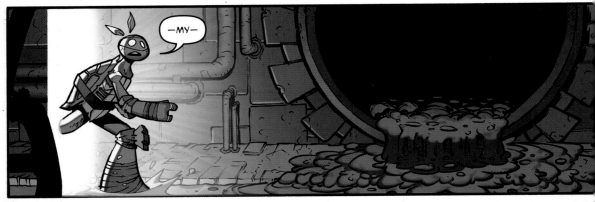

—MY—

—GULP.

DID YOU JUST SAY THE WORD "GULP"?

OH, MAN, THIS IS AWFUL. I MEAN, IT'S AWESOME, BUT ALSO MOSTLY AWFUL.

YOU GOTTA TAKE ME BACK! RIGHT THIS SECOND!

MIKEY, JUST CALM DOWN AND—

—JUST NO CHANCE THAT THE LASER RIFLE THE NEWTRALIZER WAS USING COULD BE THAT EFFECTIVE WITHOUT A BATTERY PACK AT LEAST THREE TIMES THE SIZE.

EEP! HIDE!

I'M GONNA SAY THIS IN THE NICEST WAY POSSIBLE IN ORDER TO SPARE YOUR FEELINGS, DONNIE.

NO ONE CARES. NO ONE. NOT A SINGLE LIVING PERSON.

RENET, YOU DON'T UNDERSTAND. THIS DAY. THE DAY WE'RE IN RIGHT NOW?

IT'S THE FUNNIEST DAY OF MY LIFE, BUT IT'S ALSO THE SCARIEST.

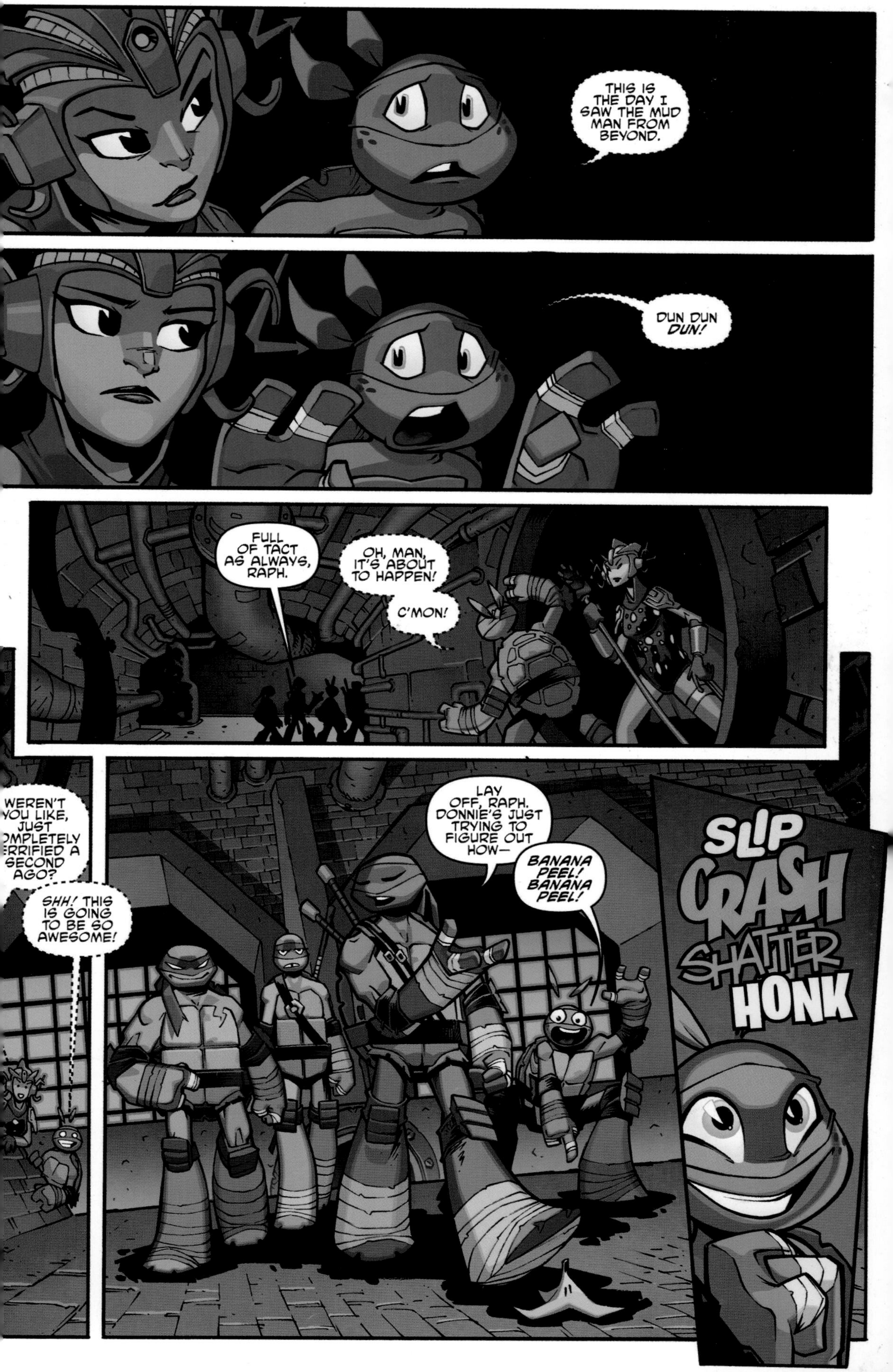
THIS IS THE DAY I SAW THE MUD MAN FROM BEYOND.
DUN DUN *DUN!*
FULL OF TACT AS ALWAYS, RAPH.
OH, MAN, IT'S ABOUT TO HAPPEN!
C'MON!
WEREN'T YOU LIKE, JUST OMPLETELY ERRIFIED A SECOND AGO?
SHH! THIS IS GOING TO BE SO AWESOME!
LAY OFF, RAPH. DONNIE'S JUST TRYING TO FIGURE OUT HOW—
BANANA PEEL! BANANA PEEL!
SLIP
CRASH
SHATTER
HONK

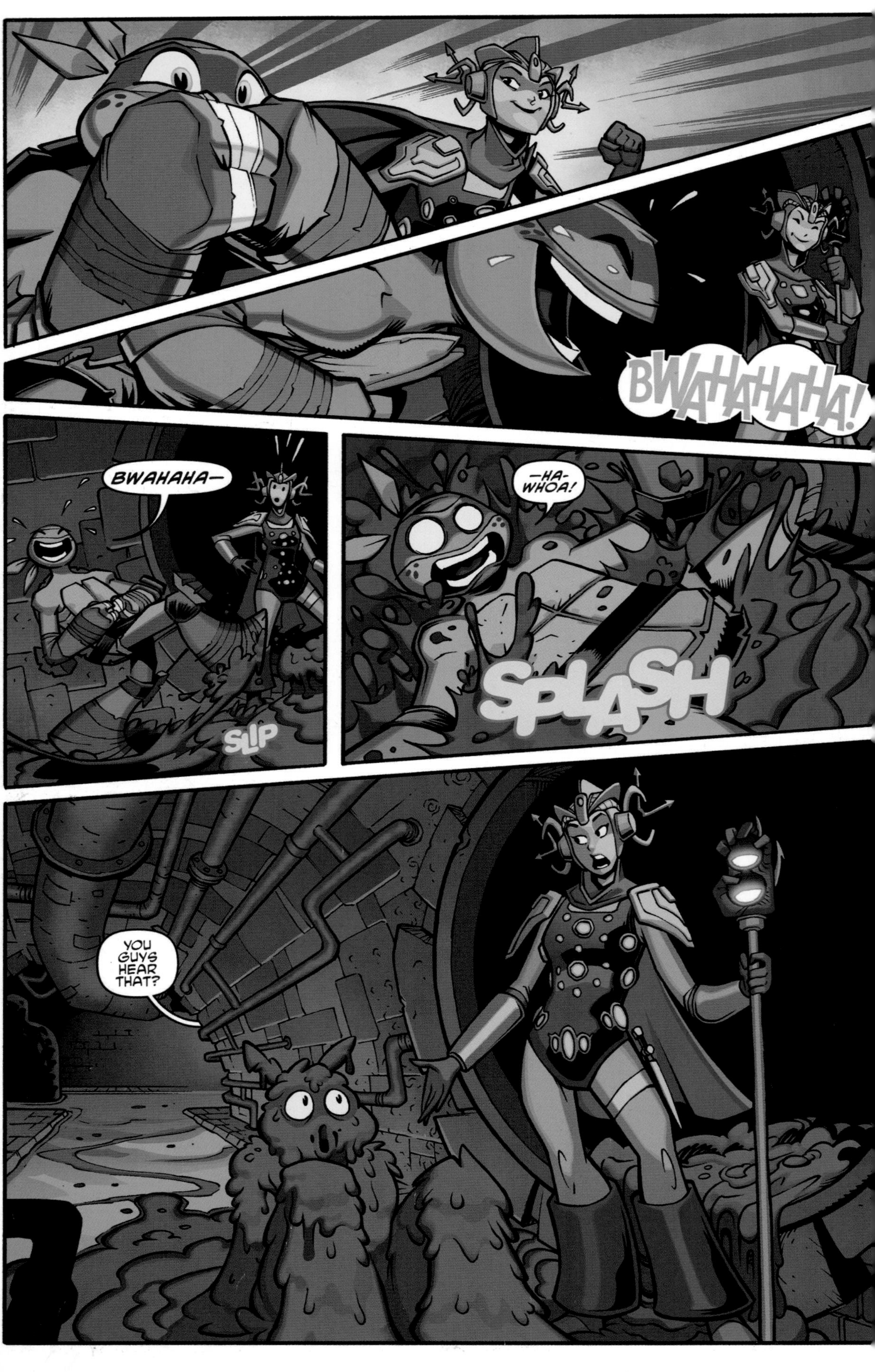
BWAHAHAHA!
BWAHAHA—
SLIP
—HA-WHOA!
SPLASH
YOU GUYS HEAR THAT?

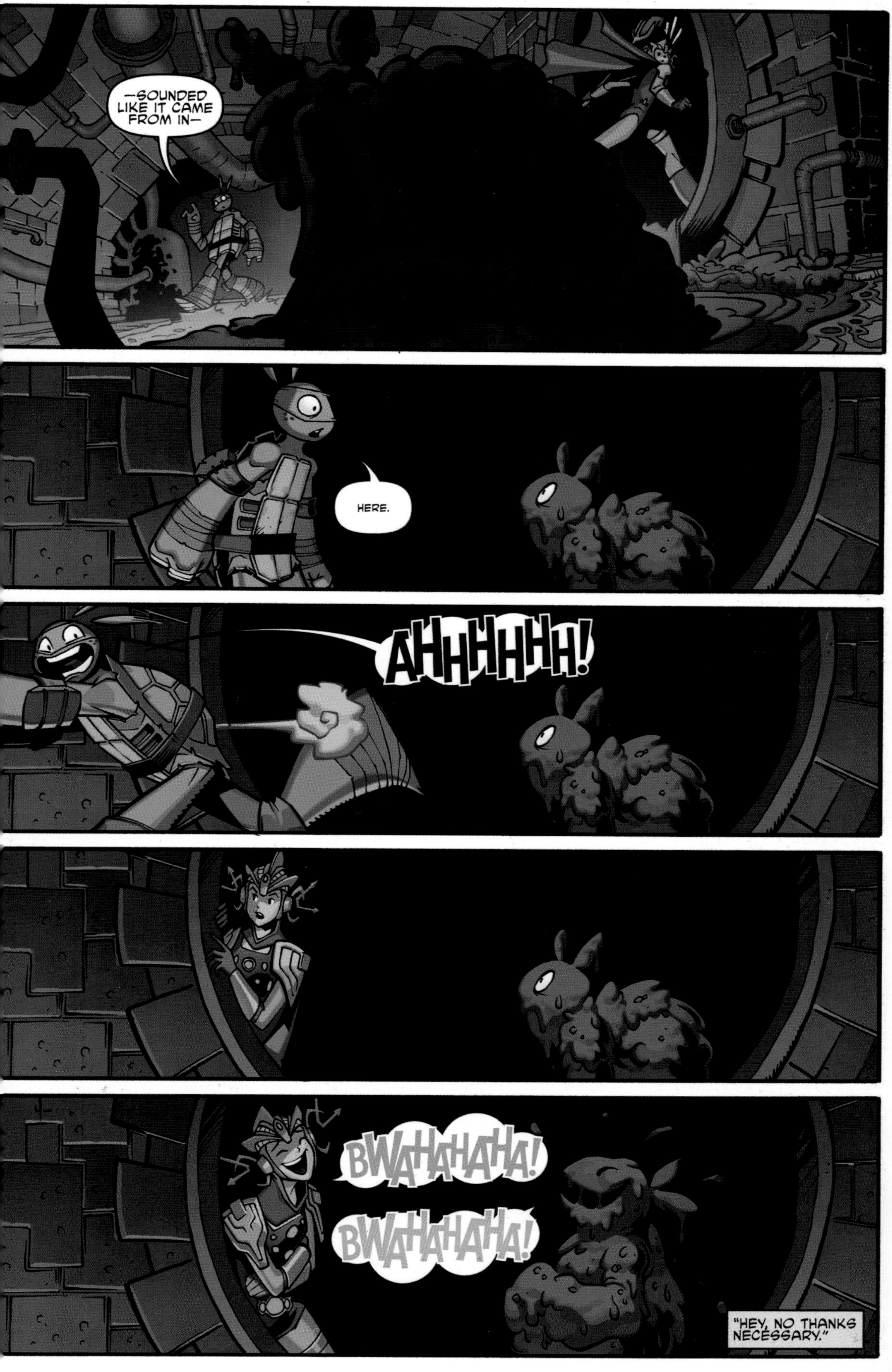
—SOUNDED LIKE IT CAME FROM IN—
HERE.
AHHHHHH!
BWAHAHAHA!
BWAHAHAHA!
"HEY, NO THANKS NECESSARY."

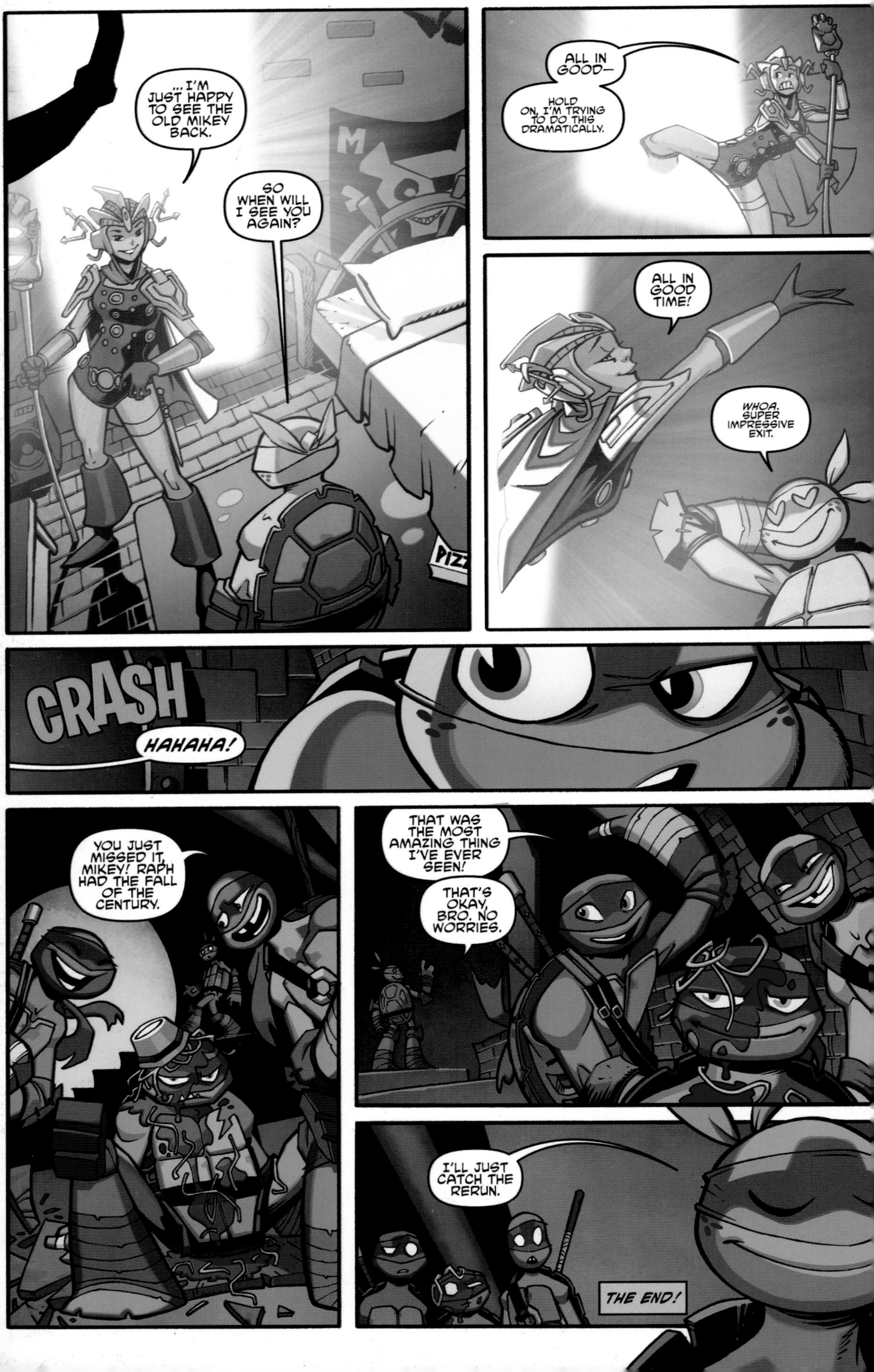
...I'M JUST HAPPY TO SEE THE OLD MIKEY BACK.
SO WHEN WILL I SEE YOU AGAIN?
ALL IN GOOD—
HOLD ON, I'M TRYING TO DO THIS DRAMATICALLY.
ALL IN GOOD TIME!
WHOA. SUPER IMPRESSIVE EXIT.
CRASH
HAHAHA!
YOU JUST MISSED IT, MIKEY! RAPH HAD THE FALL OF THE CENTURY.
THAT WAS THE MOST AMAZING THING I'VE EVER SEEN!
THAT'S OKAY, BRO. NO WORRIES.
I'LL JUST CATCH THE RERUN.
THE END!

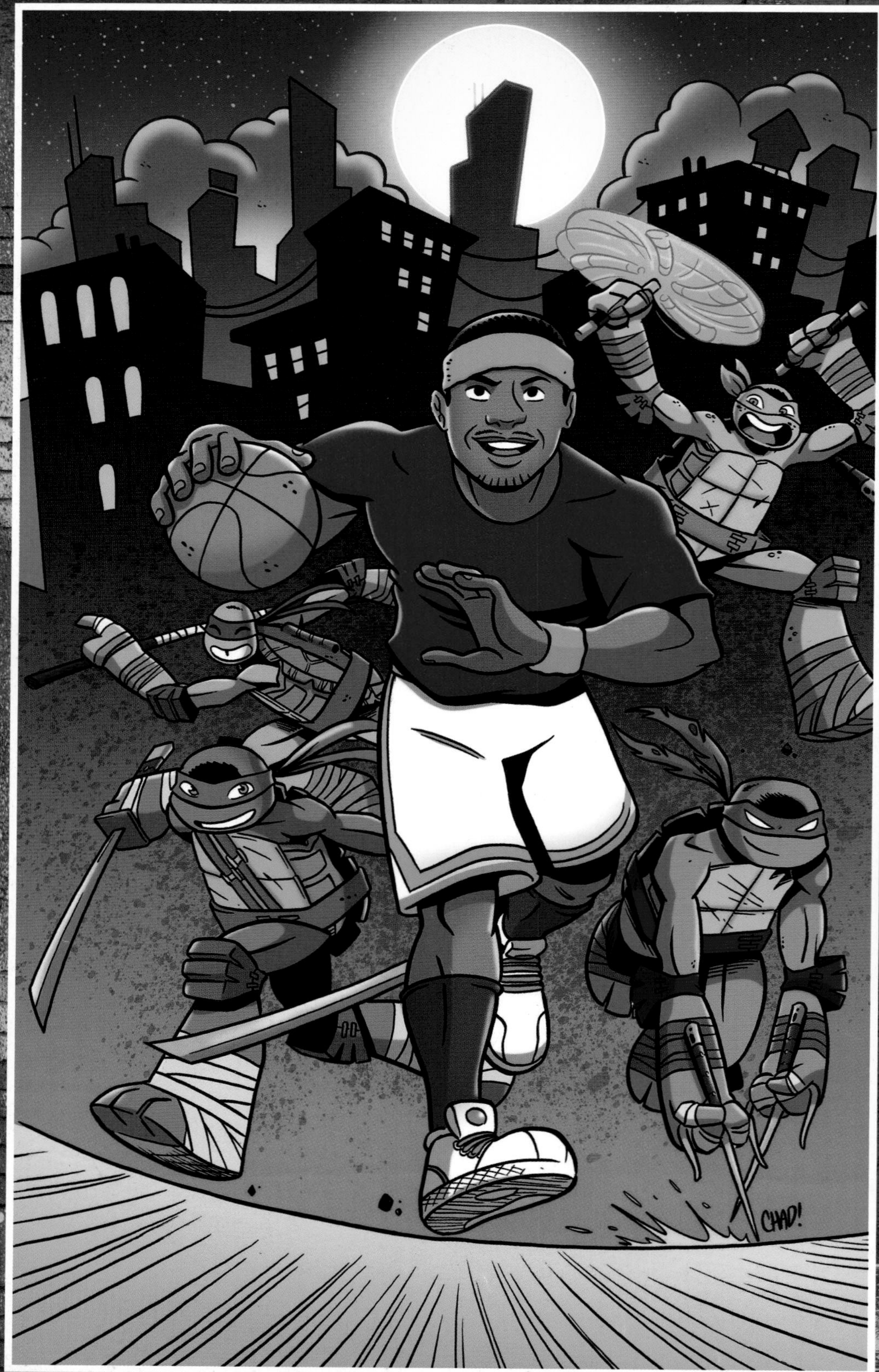
CHAD!

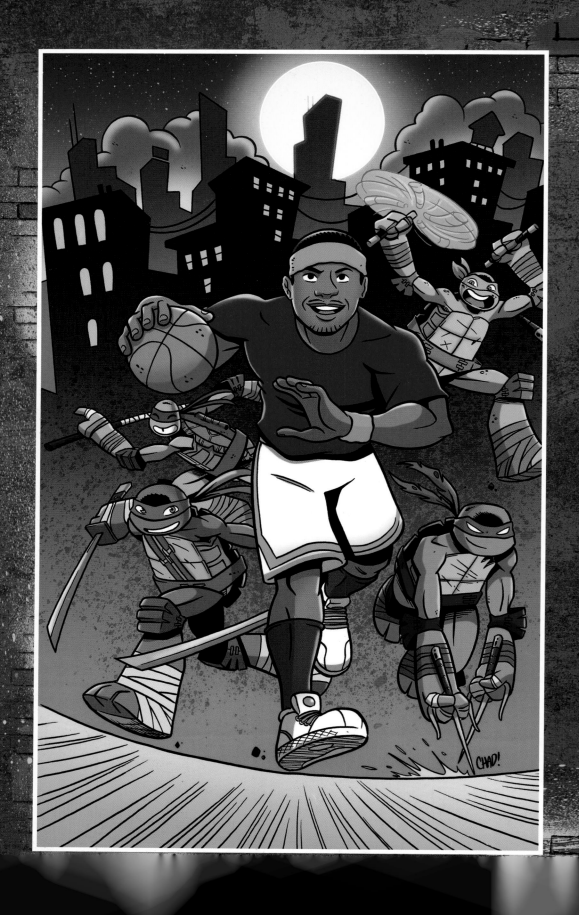

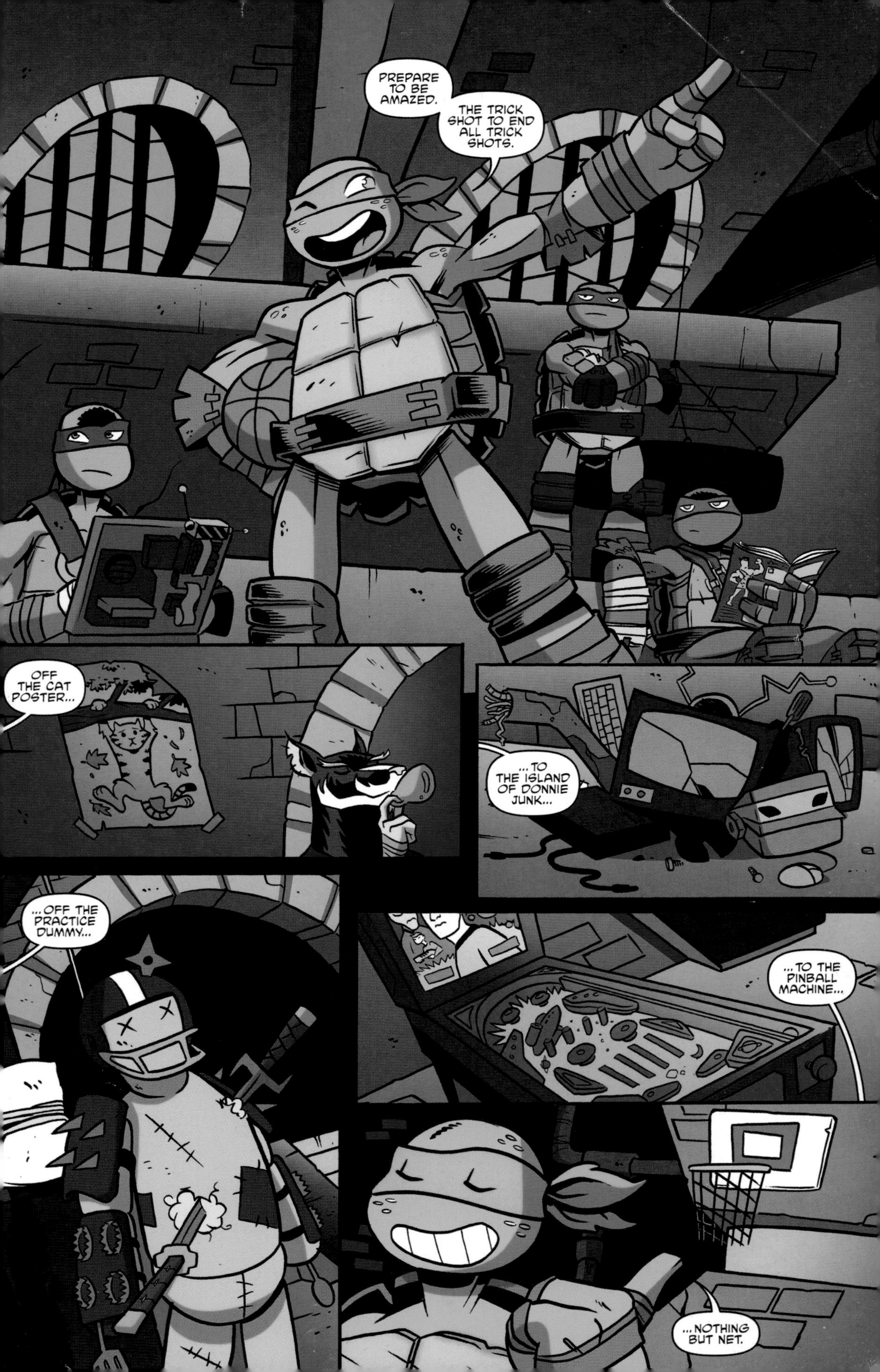
PREPARE TO BE AMAZED.
THE TRICK SHOT TO END ALL TRICK SHOTS.
OFF THE CAT POSTER...
...TO THE ISLAND OF DONNIE JUNK...
...OFF THE PRACTICE DUMMY...
...TO THE PINBALL MACHINE...
...NOTHING BUT NET.

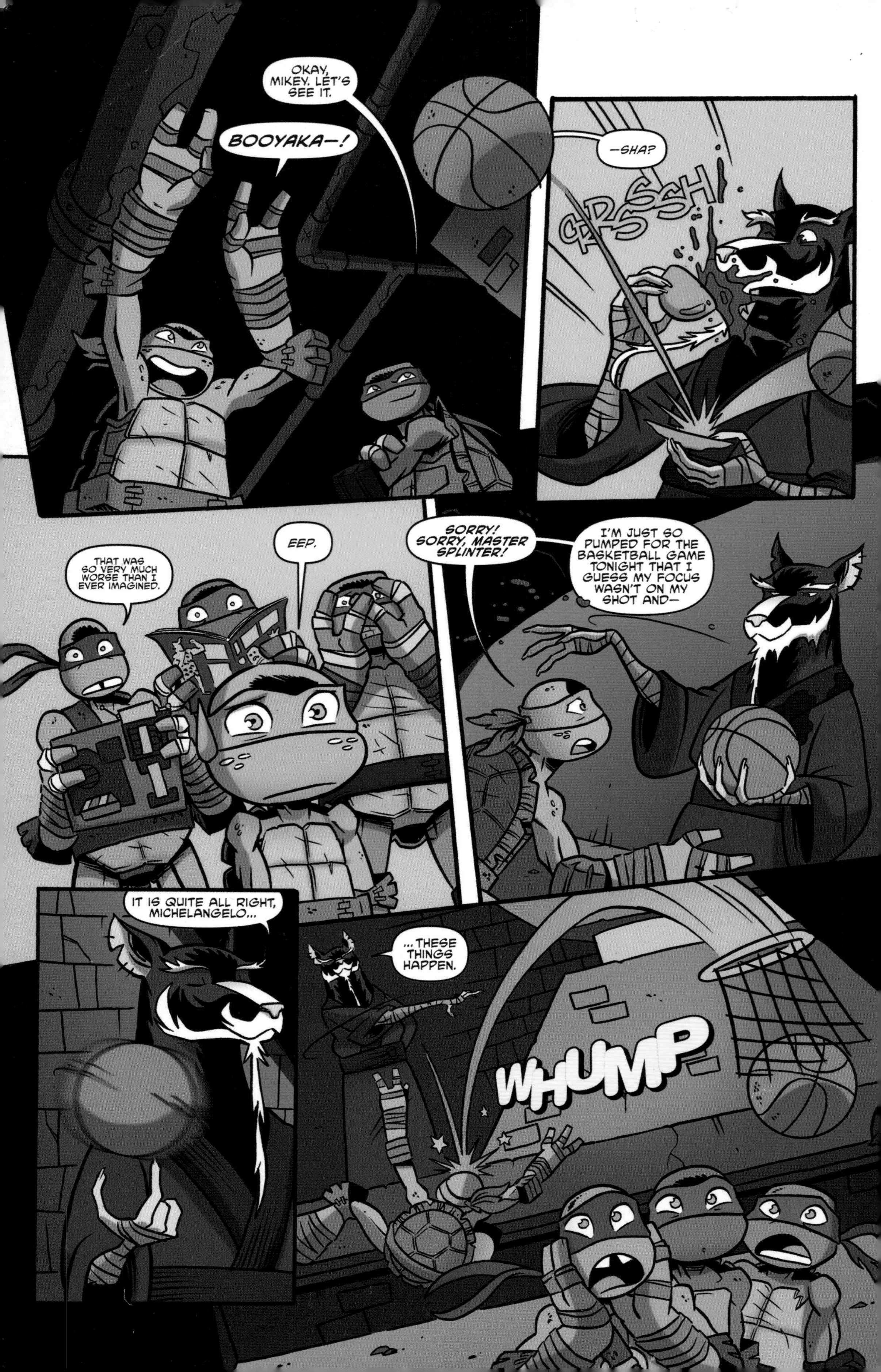

OKAY, MIKEY. LET'S SEE IT.
BOOYAKA—!
—SHA?
CRSSSH!
THAT WAS SO VERY MUCH WORSE THAN I EVER IMAGINED.
EEP.
SORRY! SORRY, MASTER SPLINTER!
I'M JUST SO PUMPED FOR THE BASKETBALL GAME TONIGHT THAT I GUESS MY FOCUS WASN'T ON MY SHOT AND—
IT IS QUITE ALL RIGHT, MICHELANGELO...
...THESE THINGS HAPPEN.
WHUMP

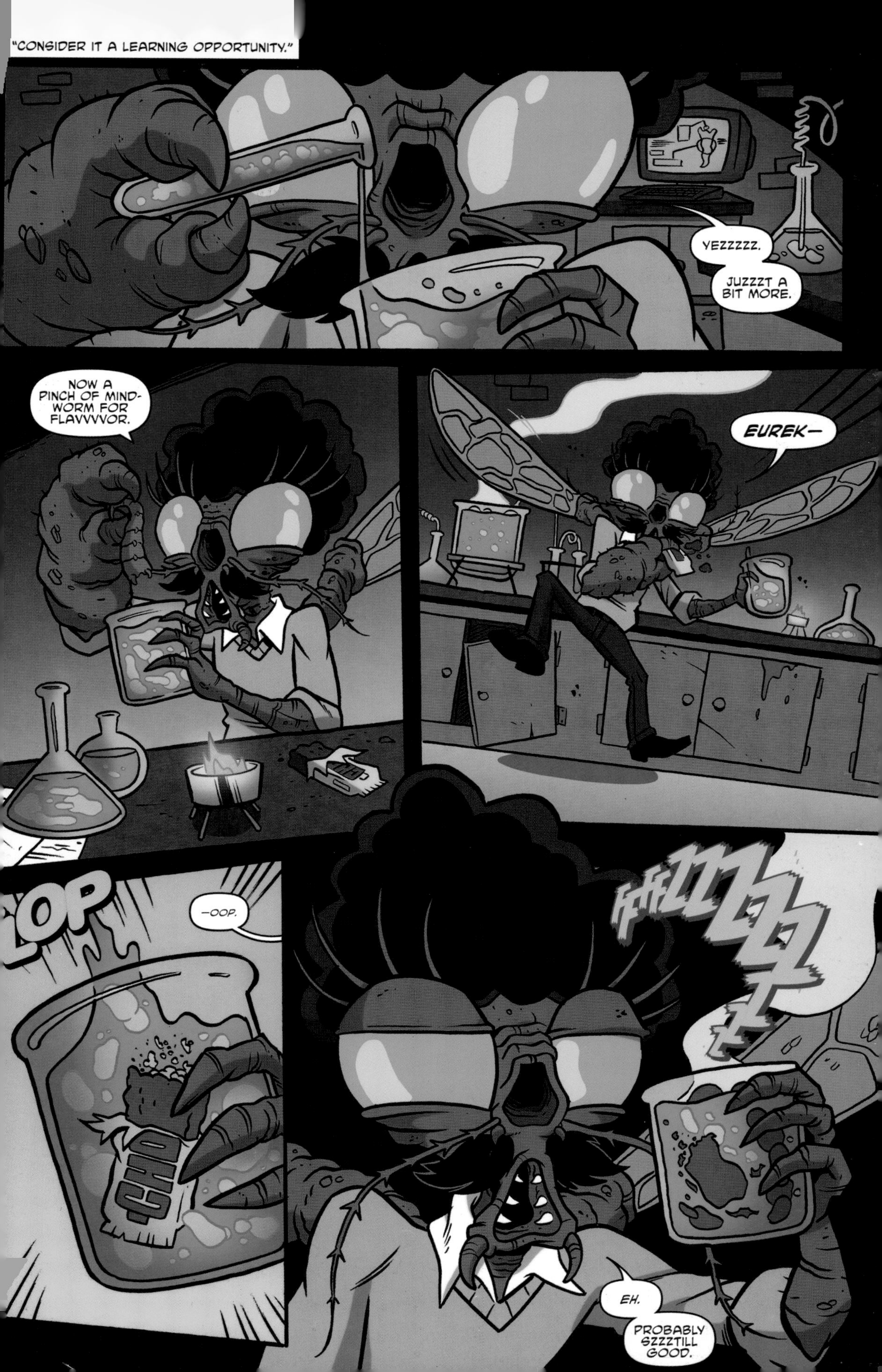
"CONSIDER IT A LEARNING OPPORTUNITY."
YEZZZZZ.
JUZZZT A BIT MORE.
NOW A PINCH OF MIND-WORM FOR FLAVVVVOR.
EUREK—
LOP
—OOP.
EH.
PROBABLY SZZZTILL GOOD.

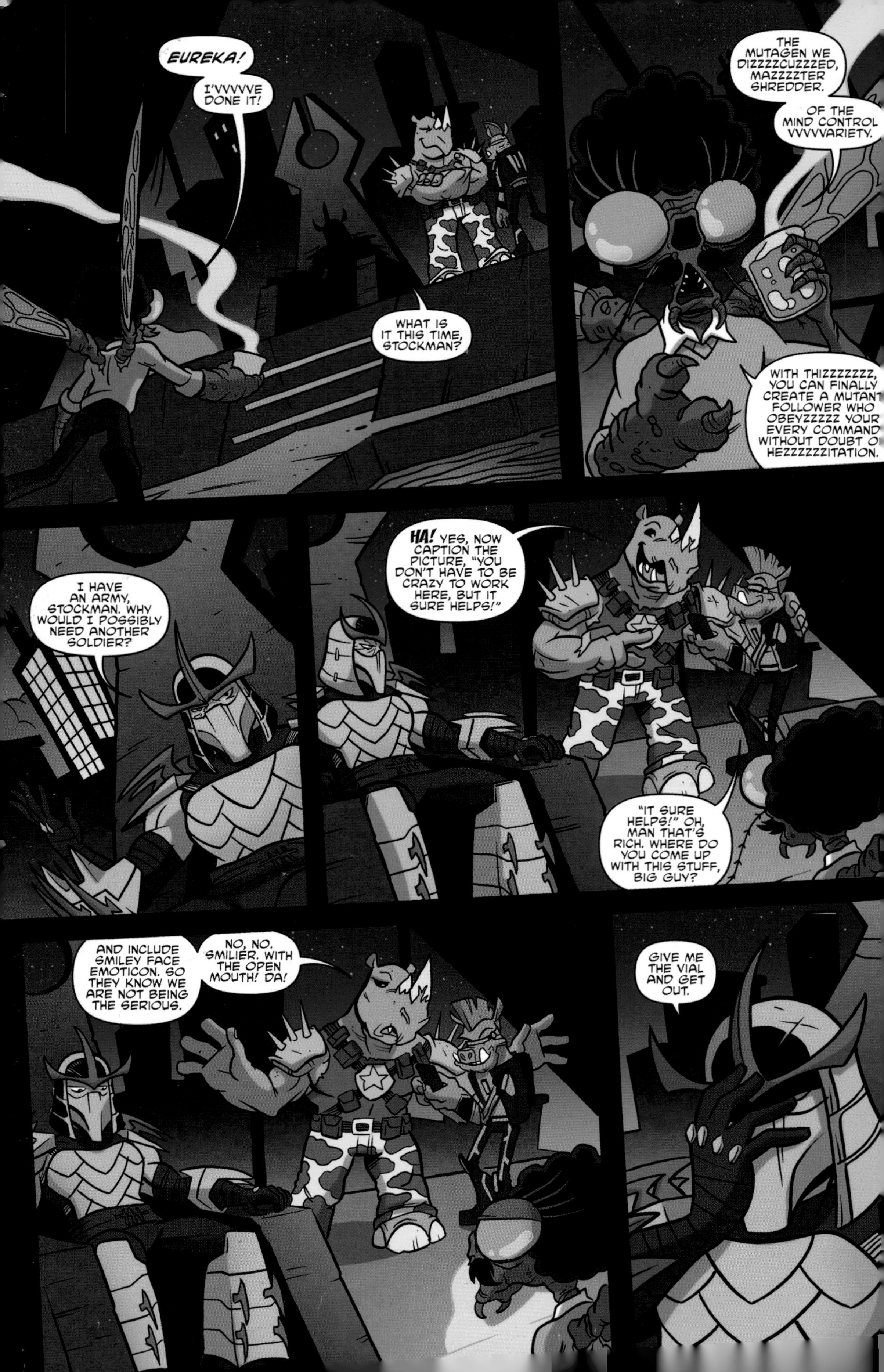
EUREKA!
I'VVVVVE DONE IT!
WHAT IS IT THIS TIME, STOCKMAN?
THE MUTAGEN WE DIZZZZCUZZZED, MAZZZZTER SHREDDER.
OF THE MIND CONTROL VVVVVARIETY.
WITH THIZZZZZZZ, YOU CAN FINALLY CREATE A MUTANT FOLLOWER WHO OBEYZZZZZ YOUR EVERY COMMAND WITHOUT DOUBT OR HEZZZZZZITATION.
I HAVE AN ARMY, STOCKMAN. WHY WOULD I POSSIBLY NEED ANOTHER SOLDIER?
HA! YES, NOW CAPTION THE PICTURE, "YOU DON'T HAVE TO BE CRAZY TO WORK HERE, BUT IT SURE HELPS!"
"IT SURE HELPS!" OH, MAN THAT'S RICH. WHERE DO YOU COME UP WITH THIS STUFF, BIG GUY?
AND INCLUDE SMILEY FACE EMOTICON. SO THEY KNOW WE ARE NOT BEING THE SERIOUS.
NO, NO. SMILIER. WITH THE OPEN MOUTH! DA!
GIVE ME THE VIAL AND GET OUT.

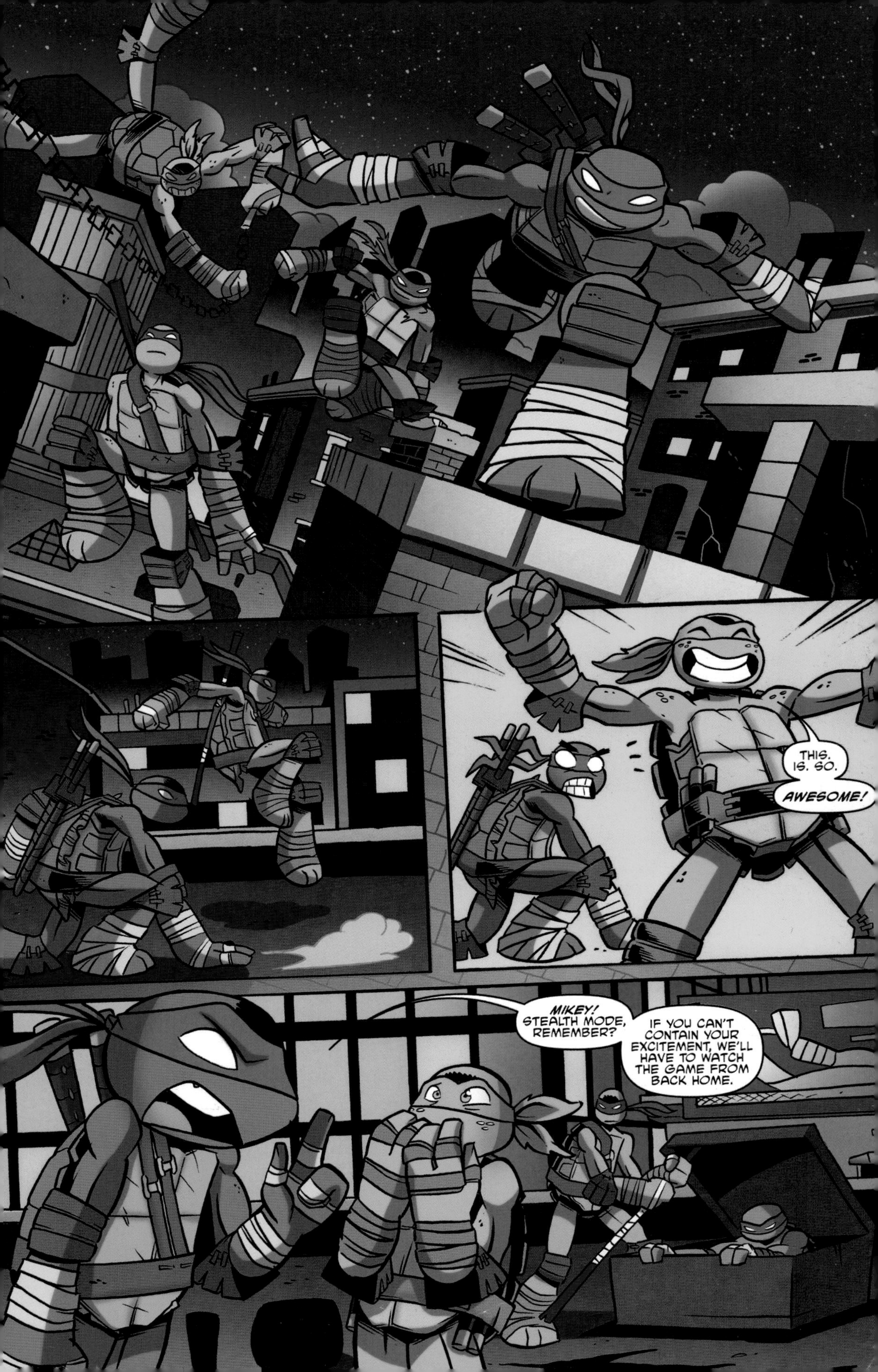
THIS. IS. SO.
AWESOME!
MIKEY! STEALTH MODE, REMEMBER?
IF YOU CAN'T CONTAIN YOUR EXCITEMENT, WE'LL HAVE TO WATCH THE GAME FROM BACK HOME.

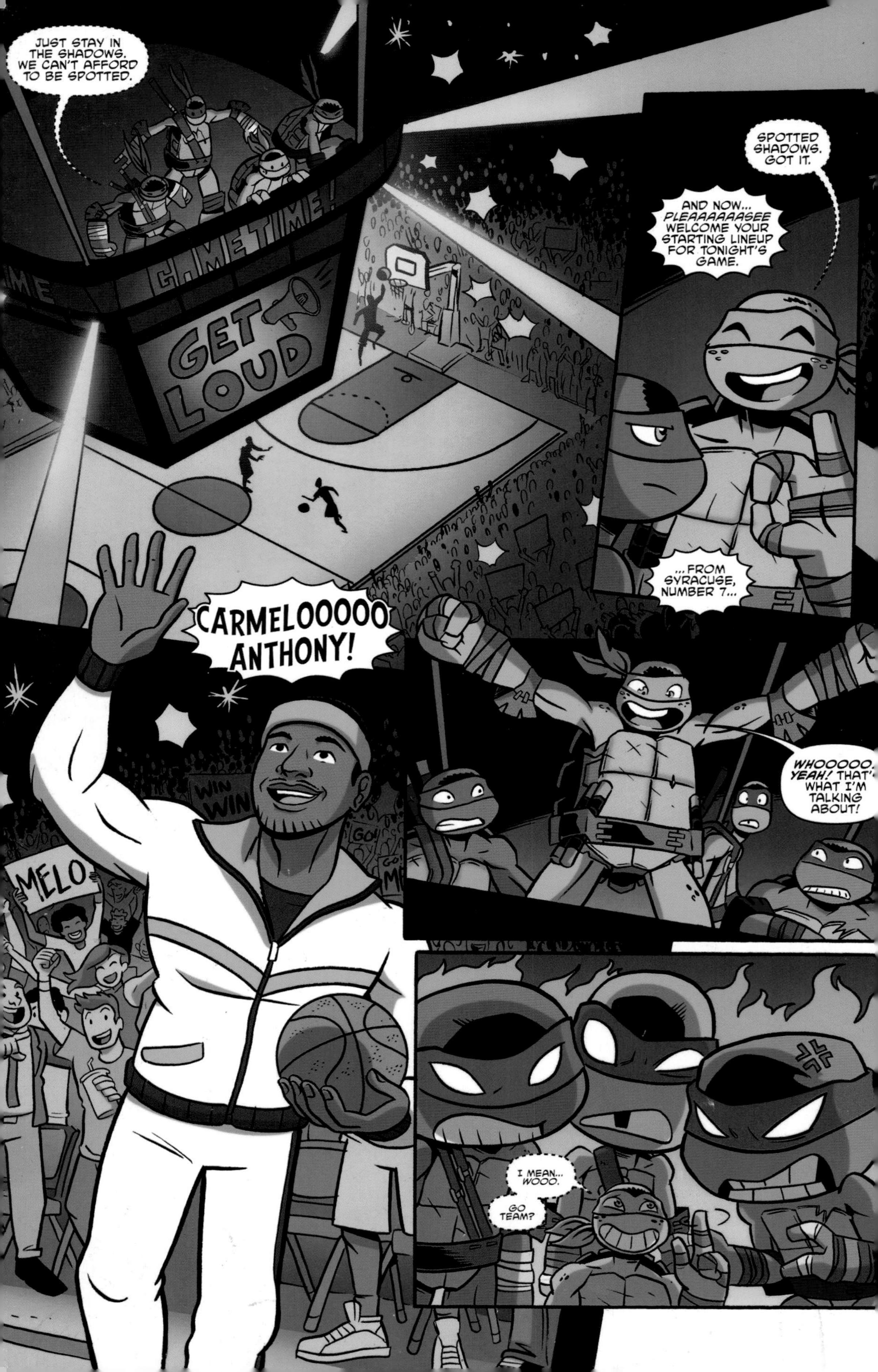
JUST STAY IN THE SHADOWS. WE CAN'T AFFORD TO BE SPOTTED.
SPOTTED SHADOWS. GOT IT.
AND NOW... PLEAAAAAASEE WELCOME YOUR STARTING LINEUP FOR TONIGHT'S GAME.
GAMETIME!
GET LOUD
...FROM SYRACUSE, NUMBER 7...
CARMELOOOOO ANTHONY!
WIN
MELO
WHOOOOO, YEAH! THAT'S WHAT I'M TALKING ABOUT!
I MEAN... WOOO.
GO TEAM?

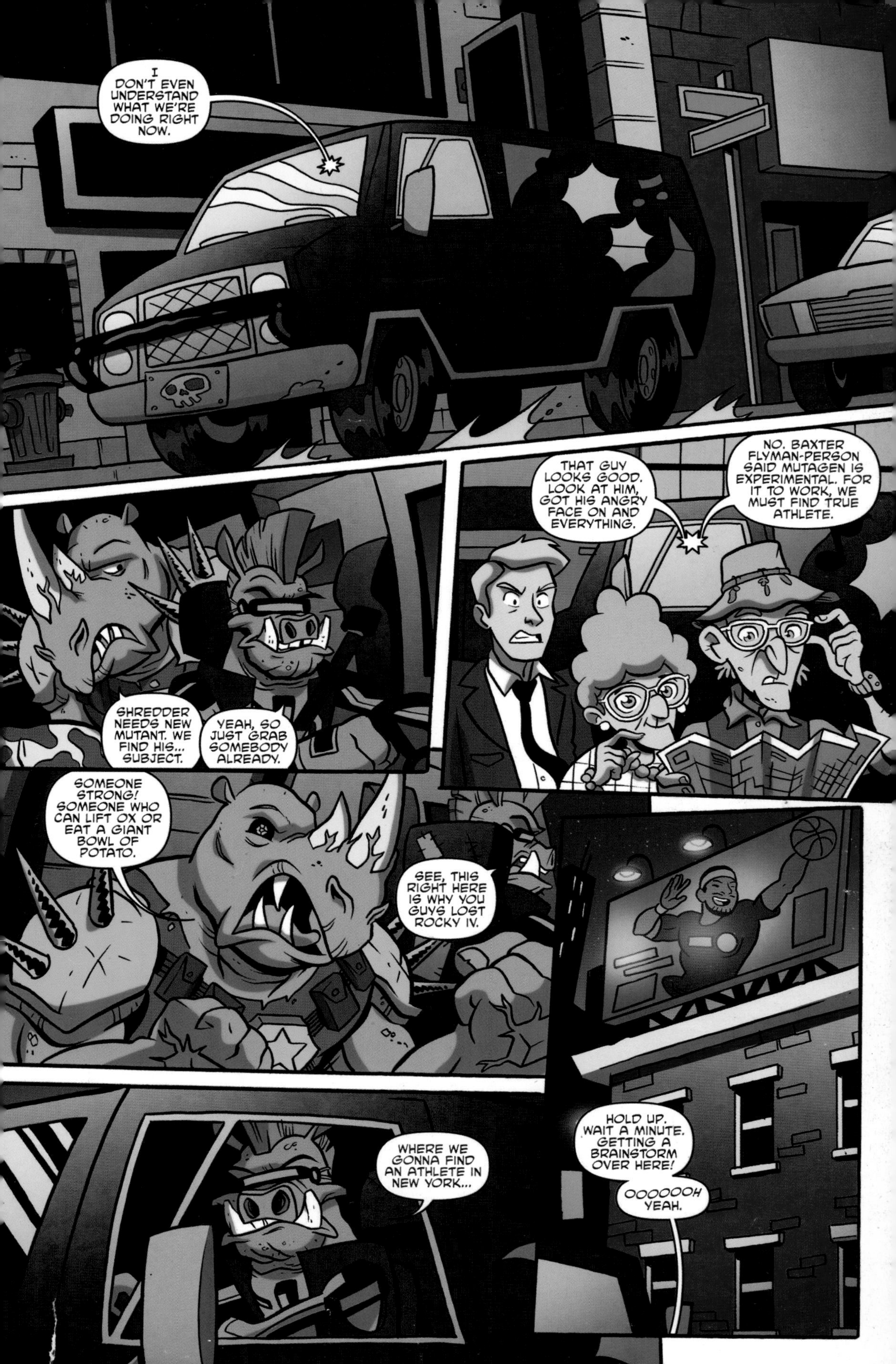
I DON'T EVEN UNDERSTAND WHAT WE'RE DOING RIGHT NOW.
SHREDDER NEEDS NEW MUTANT. WE FIND HIS... SUBJECT.
YEAH, SO JUST GRAB SOMEBODY ALREADY.
THAT GUY LOOKS GOOD. LOOK AT HIM, GOT HIS ANGRY FACE ON AND EVERYTHING.
NO. BAXTER FLYMAN-PERSON SAID MUTAGEN IS EXPERIMENTAL. FOR IT TO WORK, WE MUST FIND TRUE ATHLETE.
SOMEONE STRONG! SOMEONE WHO CAN LIFT OX OR EAT A GIANT BOWL OF POTATO.
SEE, THIS RIGHT HERE IS WHY YOU GUYS LOST ROCKY IV.
WHERE WE GONNA FIND AN ATHLETE IN NEW YORK...
HOLD UP. WAIT A MINUTE. GETTING A BRAINSTORM OVER HERE!
OOOOOOH YEAH.

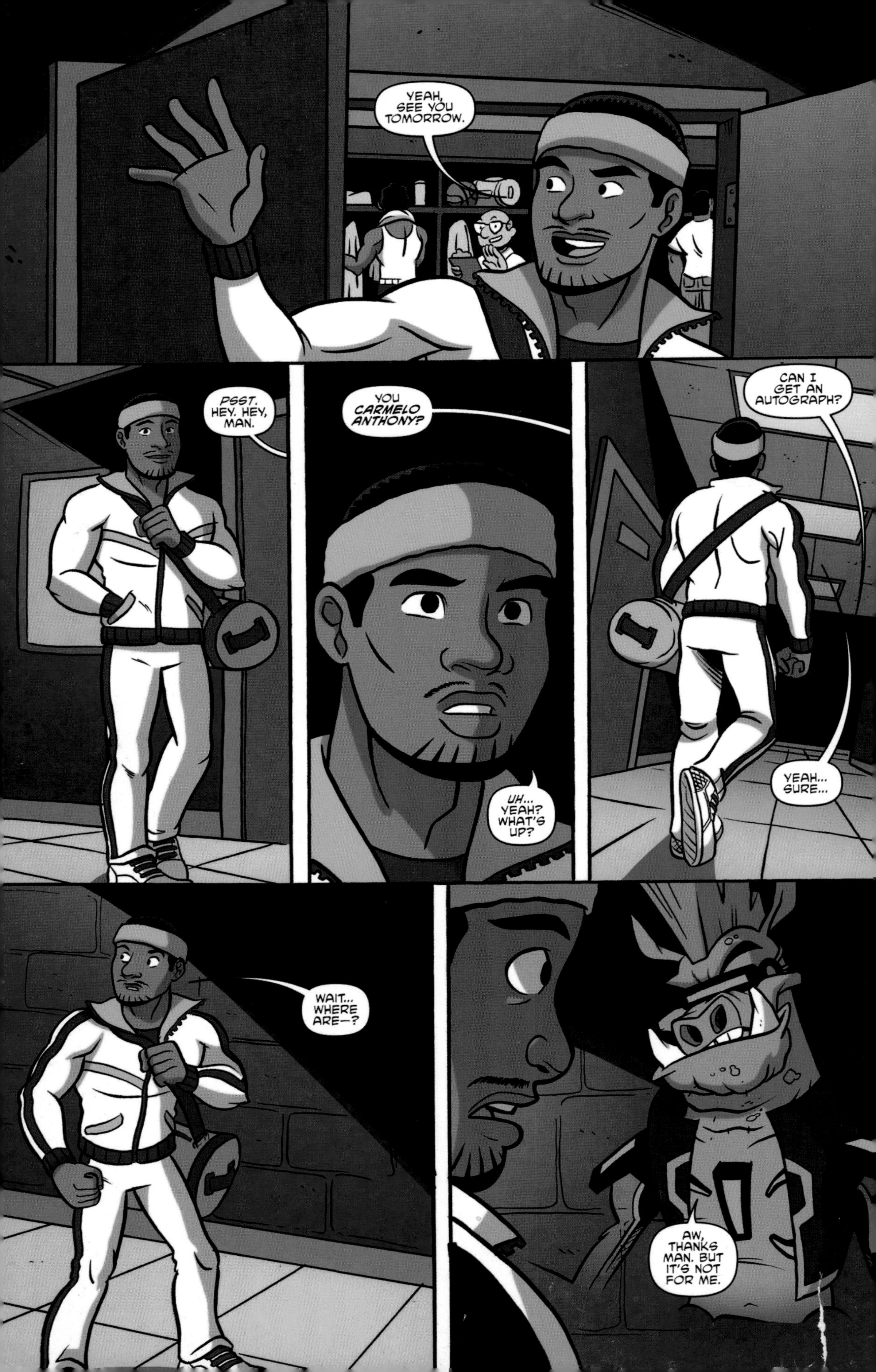
YEAH, SEE YOU TOMORROW.
PSST. HEY. HEY, MAN.
YOU CARMELO ANTHONY?
UH... YEAH? WHAT'S UP?
CAN I GET AN AUTOGRAPH?
YEAH... SURE...
WAIT... WHERE ARE--?
AW, THANKS MAN. BUT IT'S NOT FOR ME.

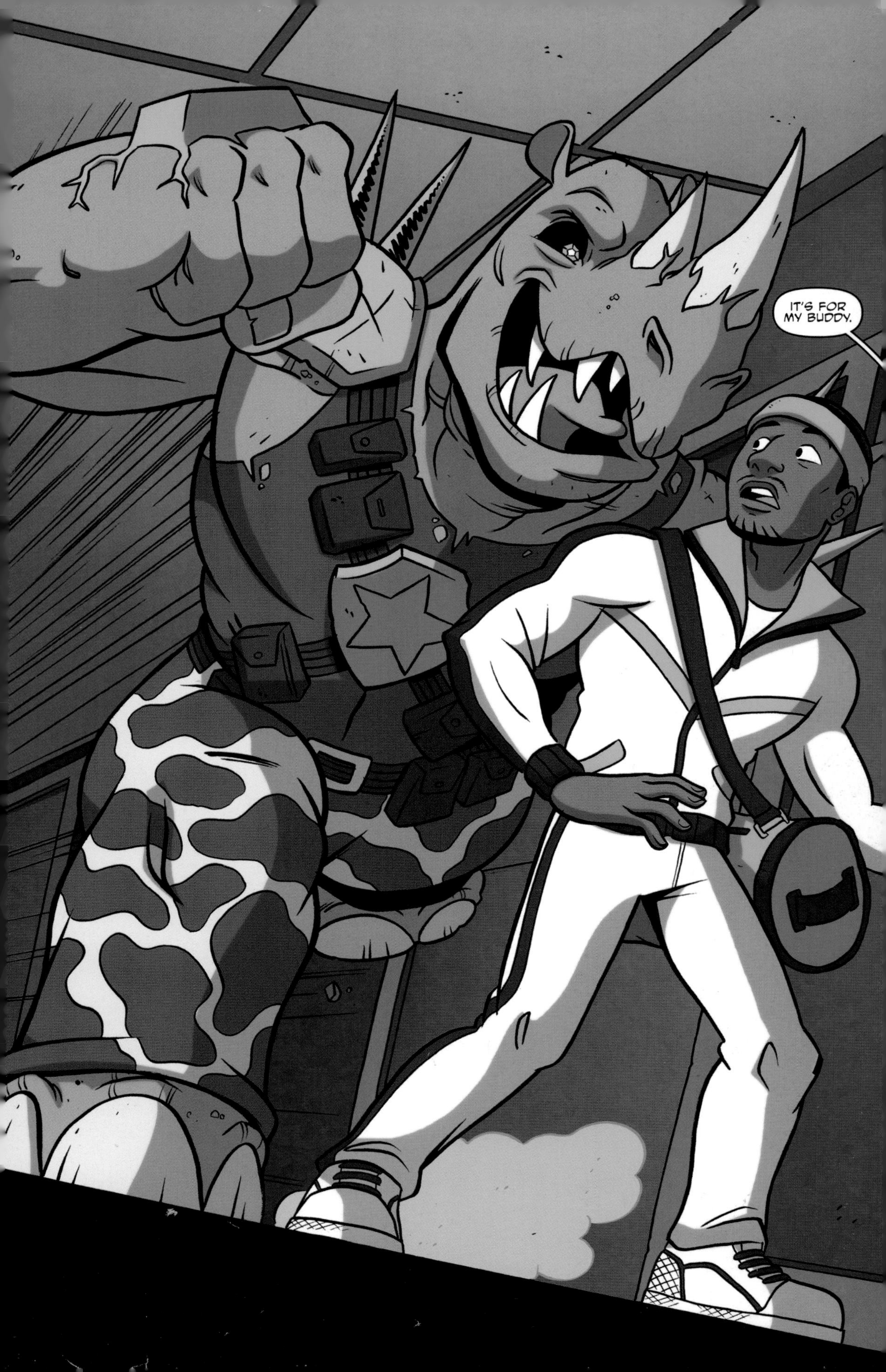
IT'S FOR MY BUDDY.

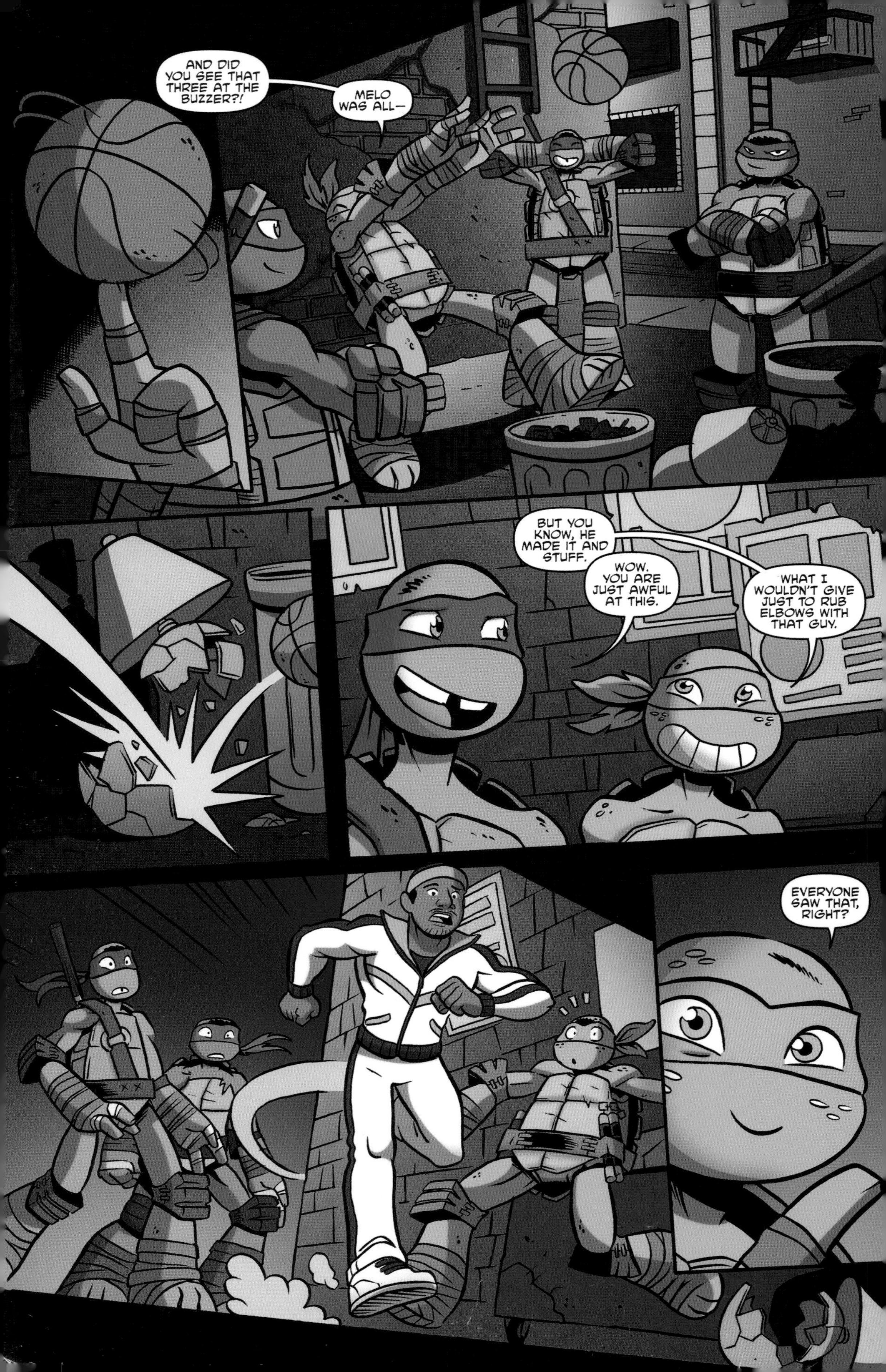
AND DID YOU SEE THAT THREE AT THE BUZZER?!
MELO WAS ALL—
BUT YOU KNOW, HE MADE IT AND STUFF.
WOW. YOU ARE JUST AWFUL AT THIS.
WHAT I WOULDN'T GIVE JUST TO RUB ELBOWS WITH THAT GUY.
EVERYONE SAW THAT, RIGHT?

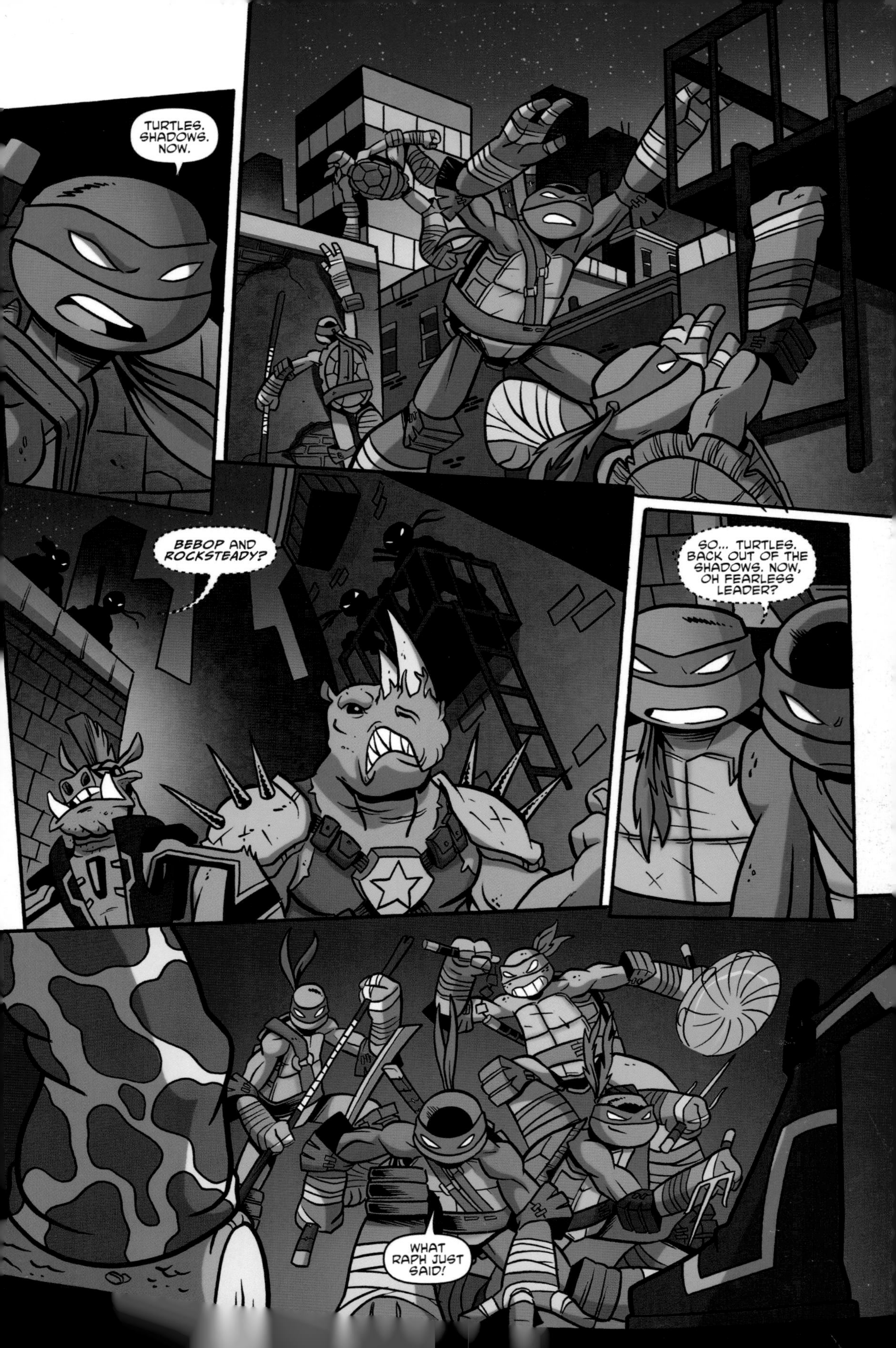
TURTLES. SHADOWS. NOW.
BEBOP AND ROCKSTEADY?
SO... TURTLES. BACK OUT OF THE SHADOWS. NOW, OH FEARLESS LEADER?
WHAT RAPH JUST SAID!

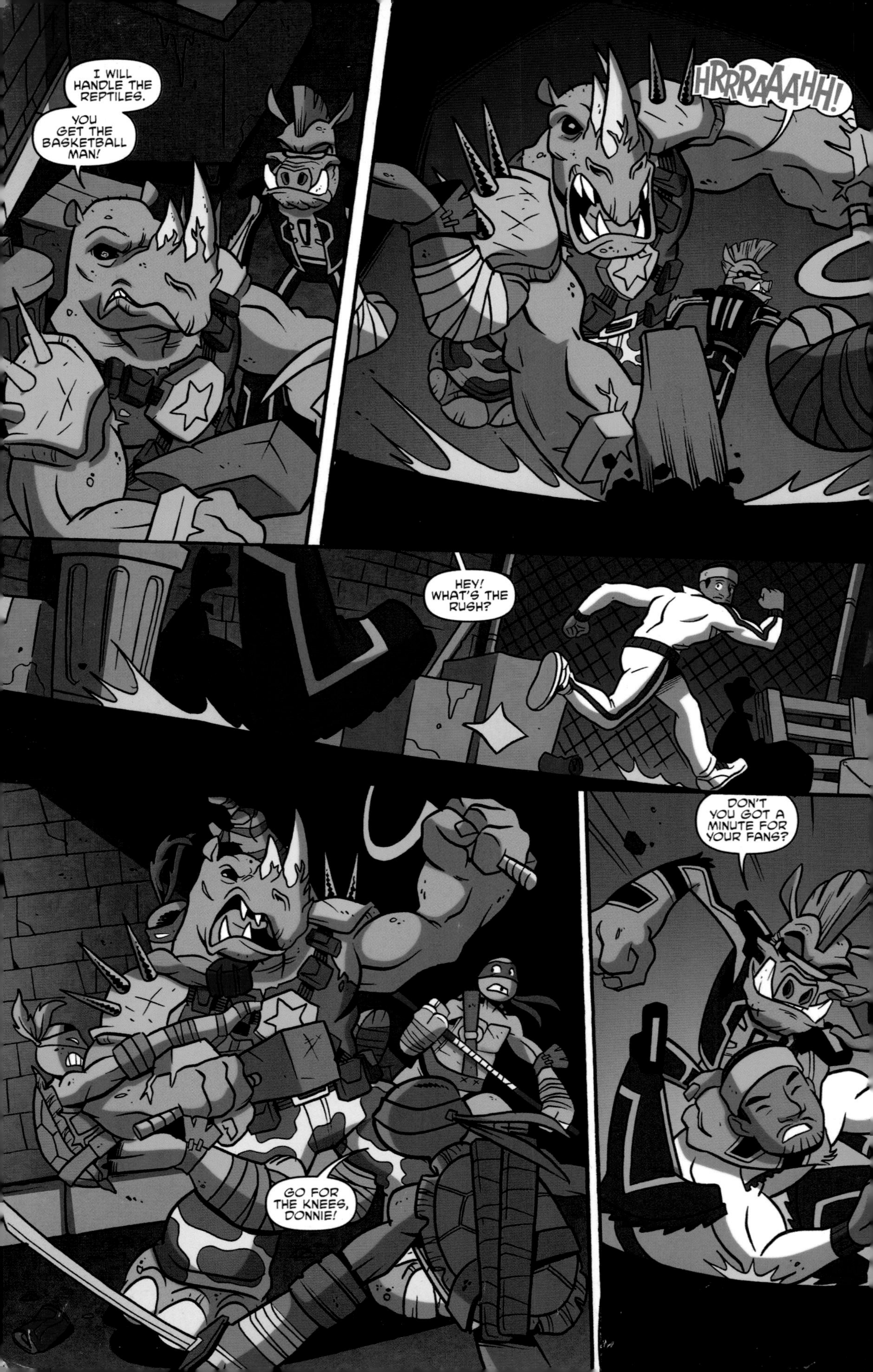
I WILL HANDLE THE REPTILES.
YOU GET THE BASKETBALL MAN!
HRRRAAAHH!
HEY! WHAT'S THE RUSH?
GO FOR THE KNEES, DONNIE!
DON'T YOU GOT A MINUTE FOR YOUR FANS?

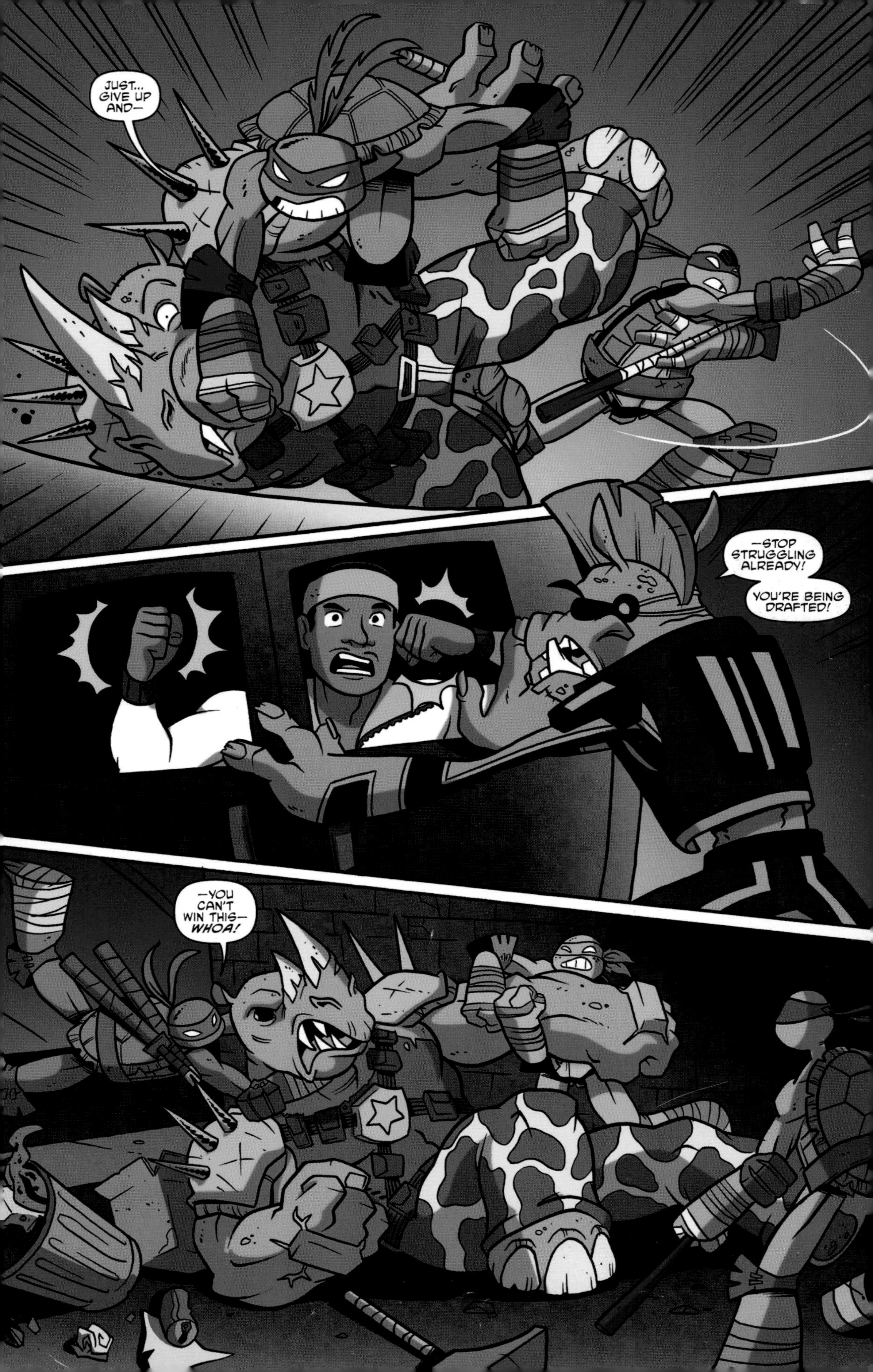
JUST... GIVE UP AND—
—STOP STRUGGLING ALREADY!
YOU'RE BEING DRAFTED!
—YOU CAN'T WIN THIS— *WHOA!*

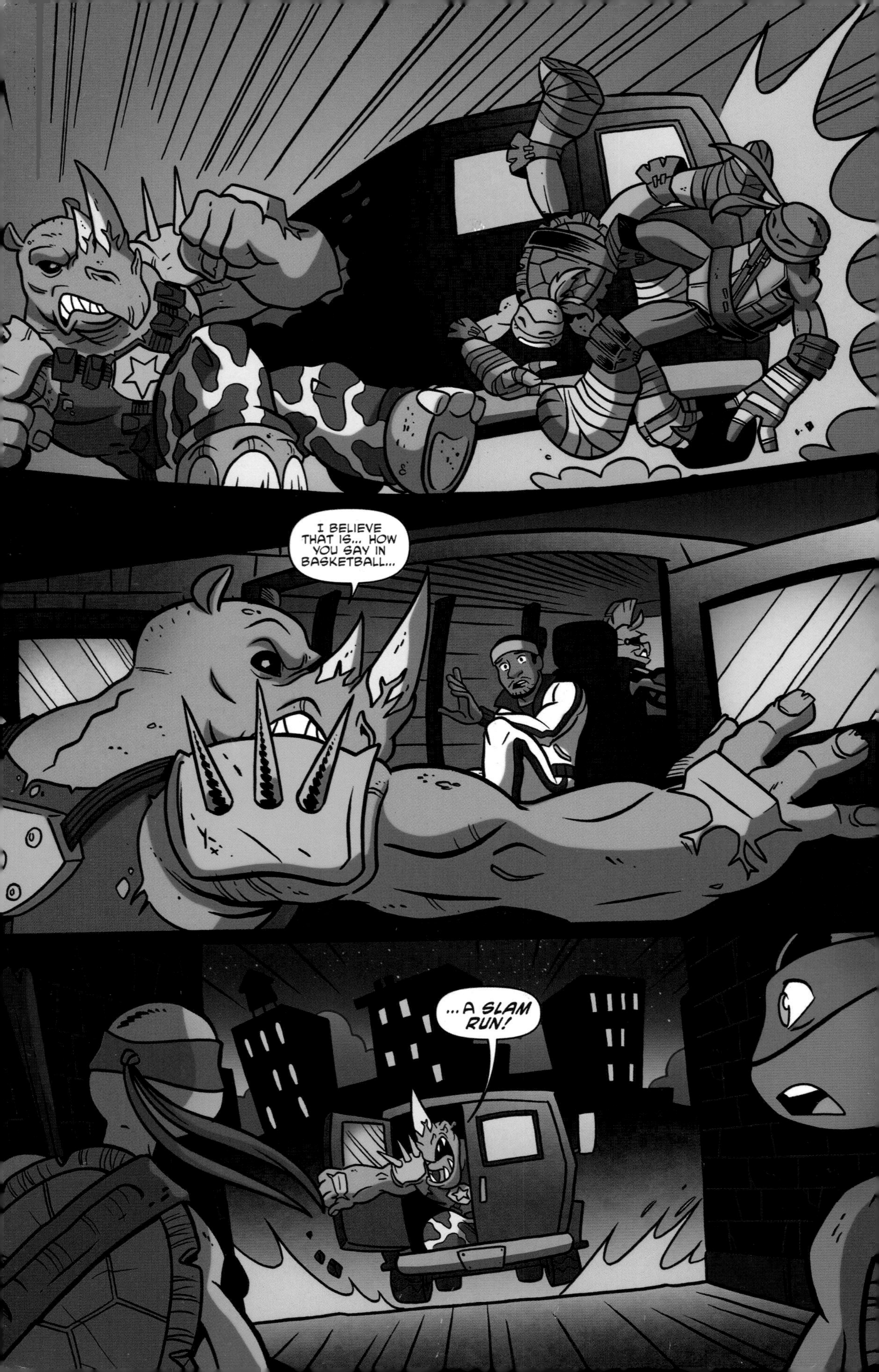
I BELIEVE THAT IS... HOW YOU SAY IN BASKETBALL...
...A SLAM RUN!

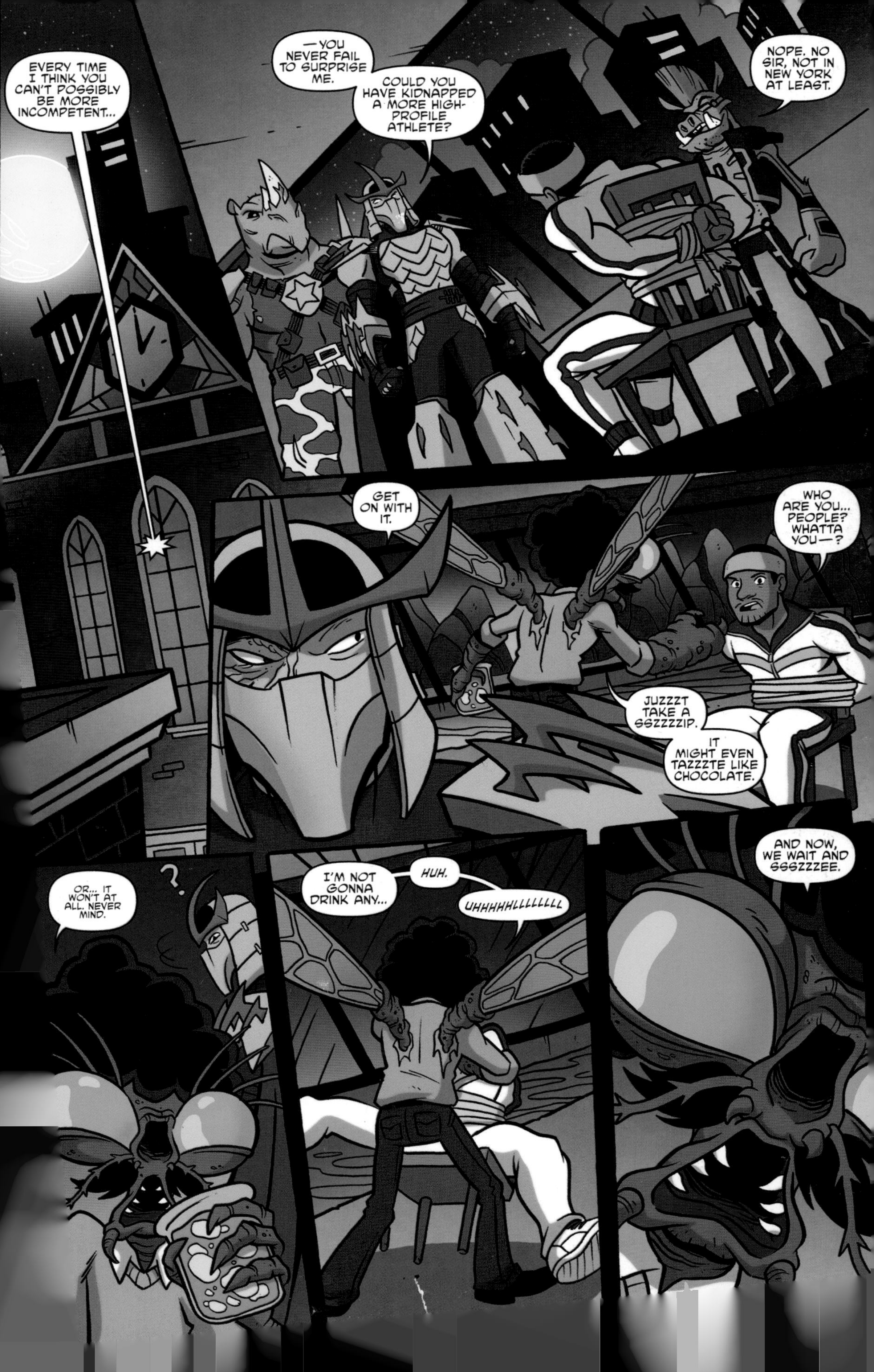
EVERY TIME I THINK YOU CAN'T POSSIBLY BE MORE INCOMPETENT...
—YOU NEVER FAIL TO SURPRISE ME.
COULD YOU HAVE KIDNAPPED A MORE HIGH-PROFILE ATHLETE?
NOPE. NO SIR, NOT IN NEW YORK AT LEAST.
GET ON WITH IT.
WHO ARE YOU... PEOPLE? WHATTA YOU—?
JUZZZT TAKE A SSZZZZIP.
IT MIGHT EVEN TAZZZTE LIKE CHOCOLATE.
?
OR... IT WON'T AT ALL. NEVER MIND.
I'M NOT GONNA DRINK ANY...
HUH.
UHHHHHLLLLLLLLL
AND NOW, WE WAIT AND SSSZZZEE.

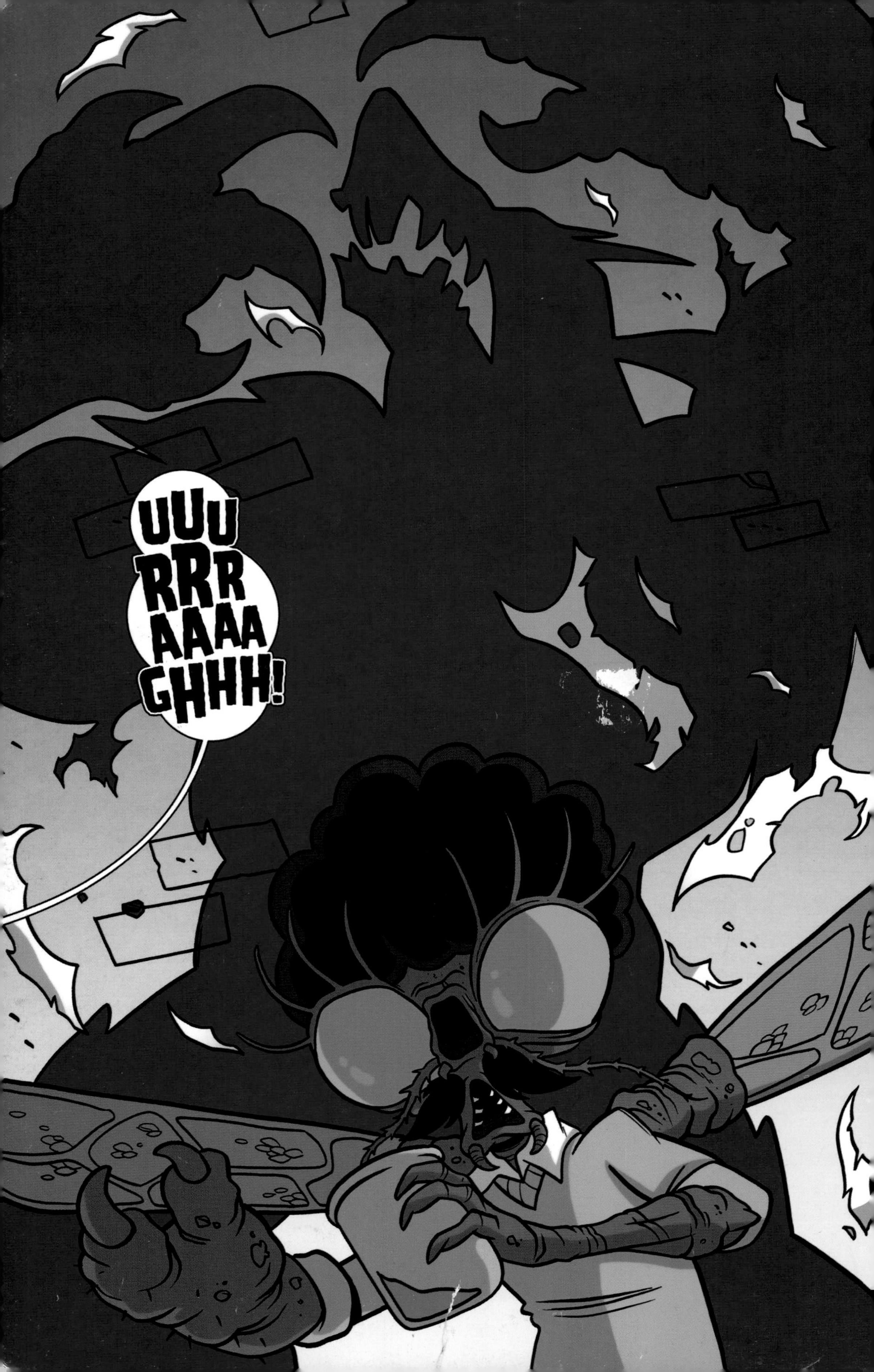
UUURRRAAAAGHHH!

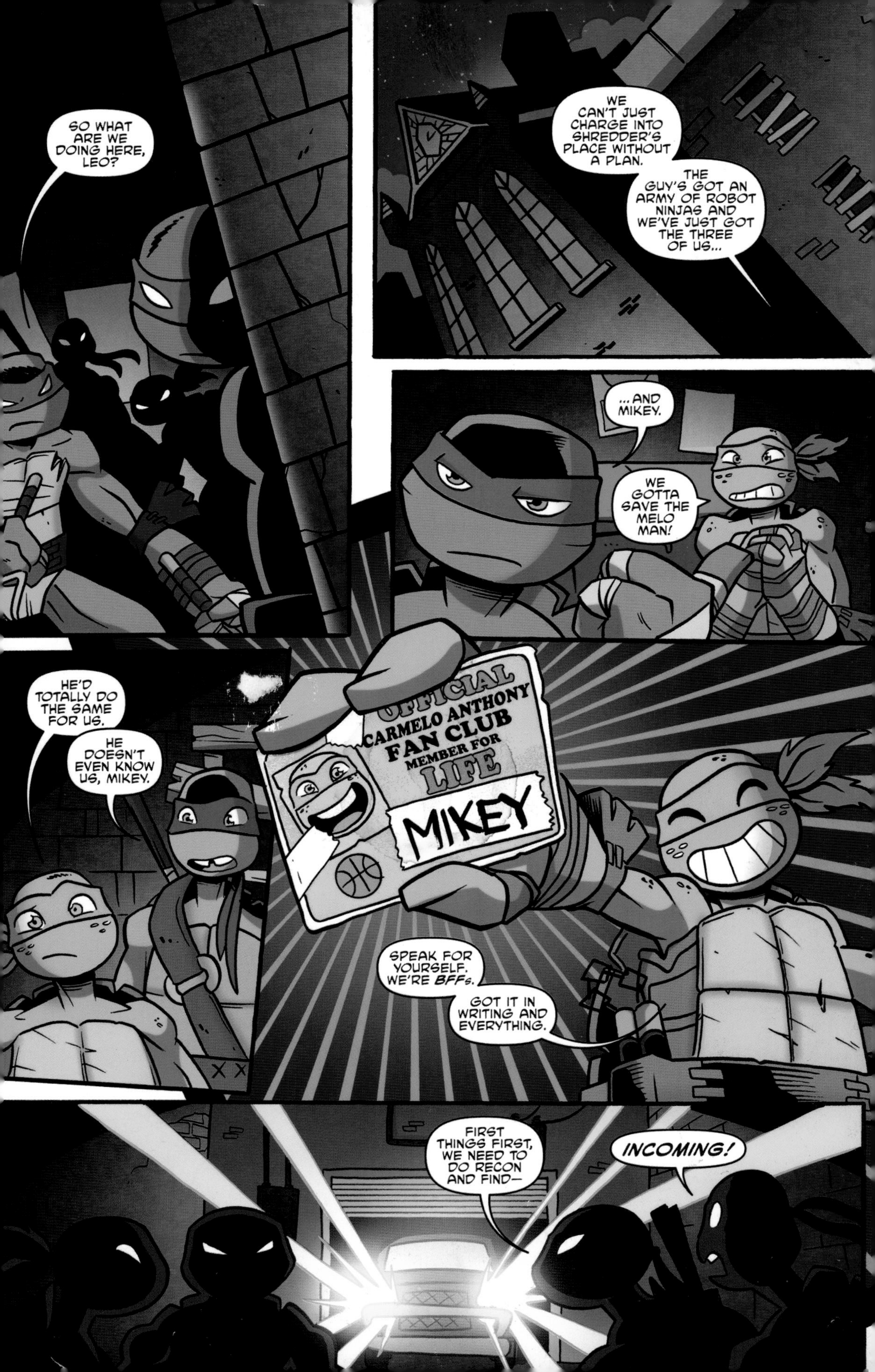
SO WHAT ARE WE DOING HERE, LEO?
WE CAN'T JUST CHARGE INTO SHREDDER'S PLACE WITHOUT A PLAN.
THE GUY'S GOT AN ARMY OF ROBOT NINJAS AND WE'VE JUST GOT THE THREE OF US...
...AND MIKEY.
WE GOTTA SAVE THE MELO MAN!
HE'D TOTALLY DO THE SAME FOR US.
HE DOESN'T EVEN KNOW US, MIKEY.
OFFICIAL CARMELO ANTHONY FAN CLUB MEMBER FOR LIFE
MIKEY
SPEAK FOR YOURSELF. WE'RE BFFs.
GOT IT IN WRITING AND EVERYTHING.
FIRST THINGS FIRST, WE NEED TO DO RECON AND FIND—
INCOMING!

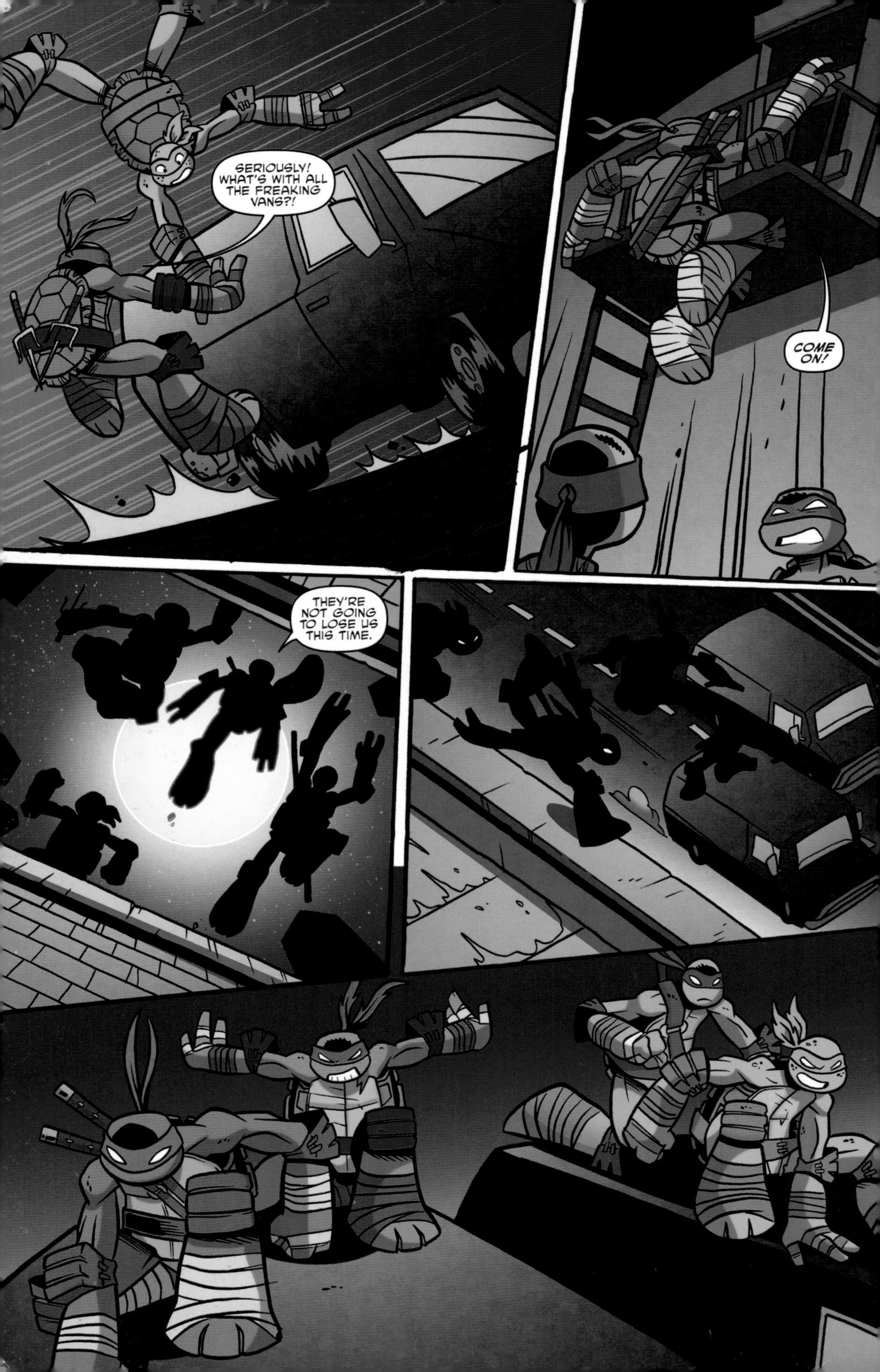
SERIOUSLY! WHAT'S WITH ALL THE FREAKING VANS?!
COME ON!
THEY'RE NOT GOING TO LOSE US THIS TIME.

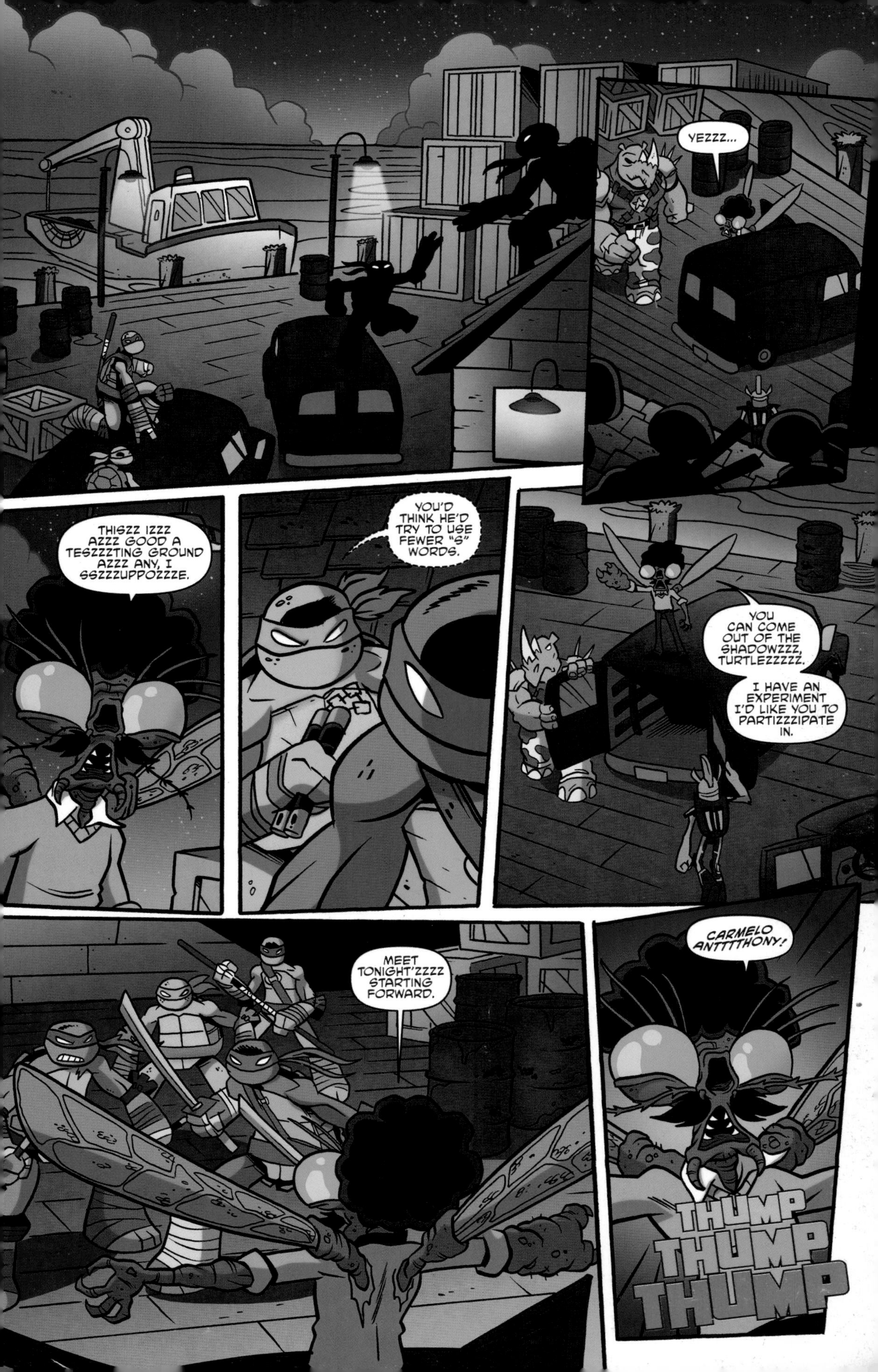
YEZZZ...
THISZZ IZZZ AZZZ GOOD A TESZZZTING GROUND AZZZ ANY, I SSZZZZUPPOZZZZE.
YOU'D THINK HE'D TRY TO USE FEWER "S" WORDS.
YOU CAN COME OUT OF THE SHADOWZZZ, TURTLEZZZZZ.
I HAVE AN EXPERIMENT I'D LIKE YOU TO PARTIZZZIPATE IN.
MEET TONIGHT'ZZZZ STARTING FORWARD.
CARMELO ANTTTTHONY!
THUMP
THUMP
THUMP

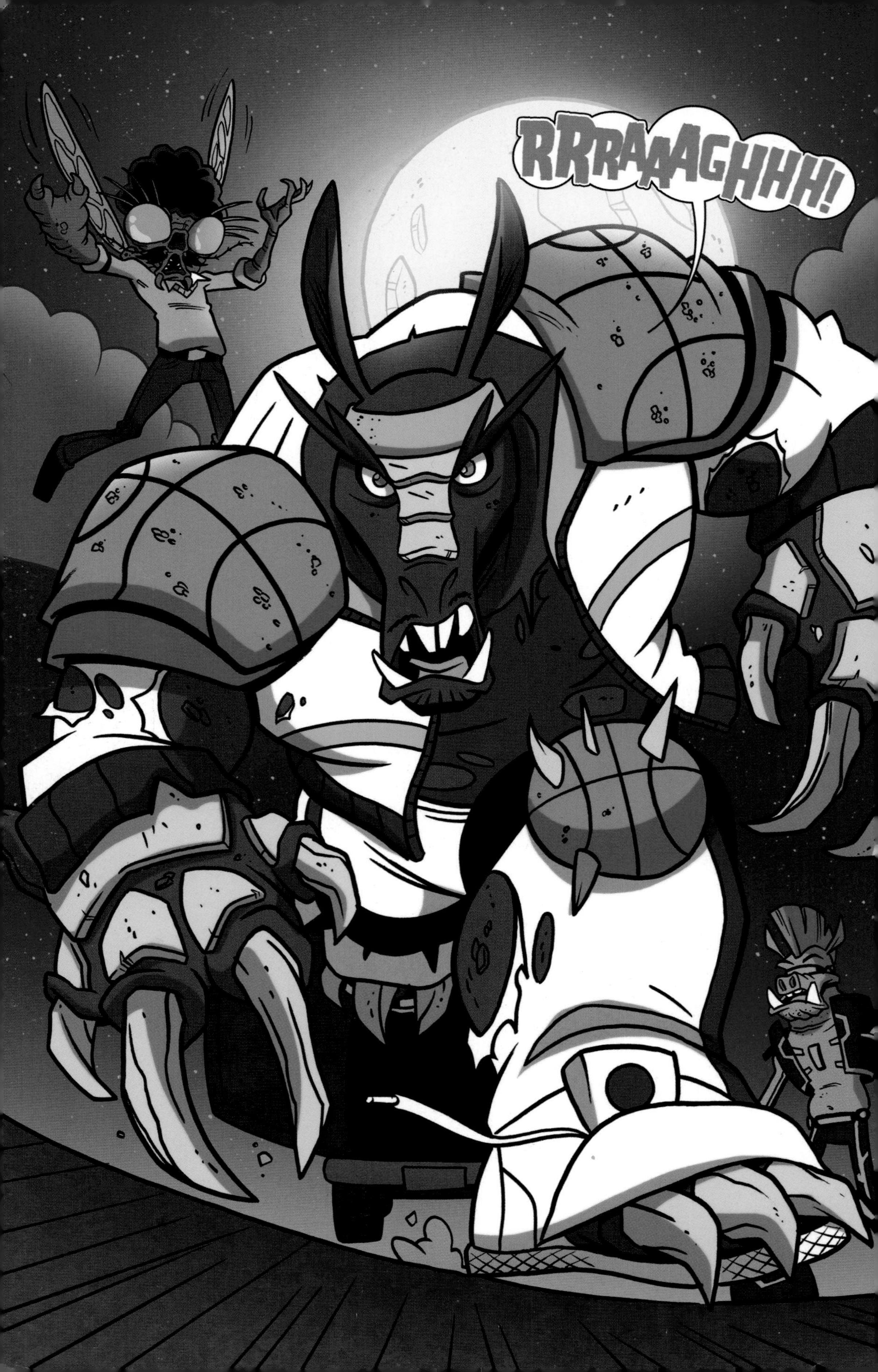
RRRAAAGHHH!

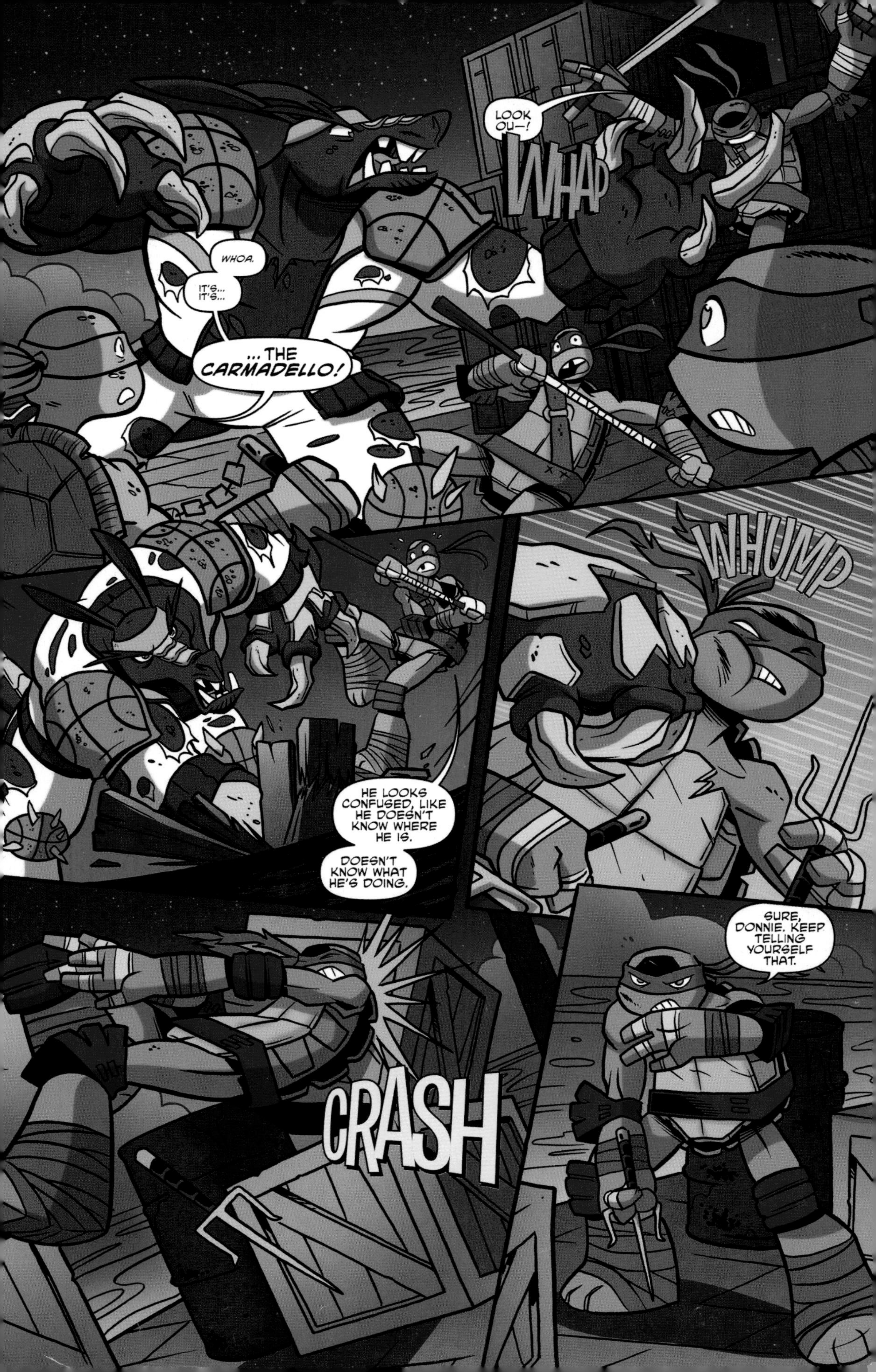

LOOK OU—!
WHAP
WHOA.
IT'S... IT'S...
...THE CARMADELLO!
WHUMP
HE LOOKS CONFUSED, LIKE HE DOESN'T KNOW WHERE HE IS.
DOESN'T KNOW WHAT HE'S DOING.
CRASH
SURE, DONNIE. KEEP TELLING YOURSELF THAT.

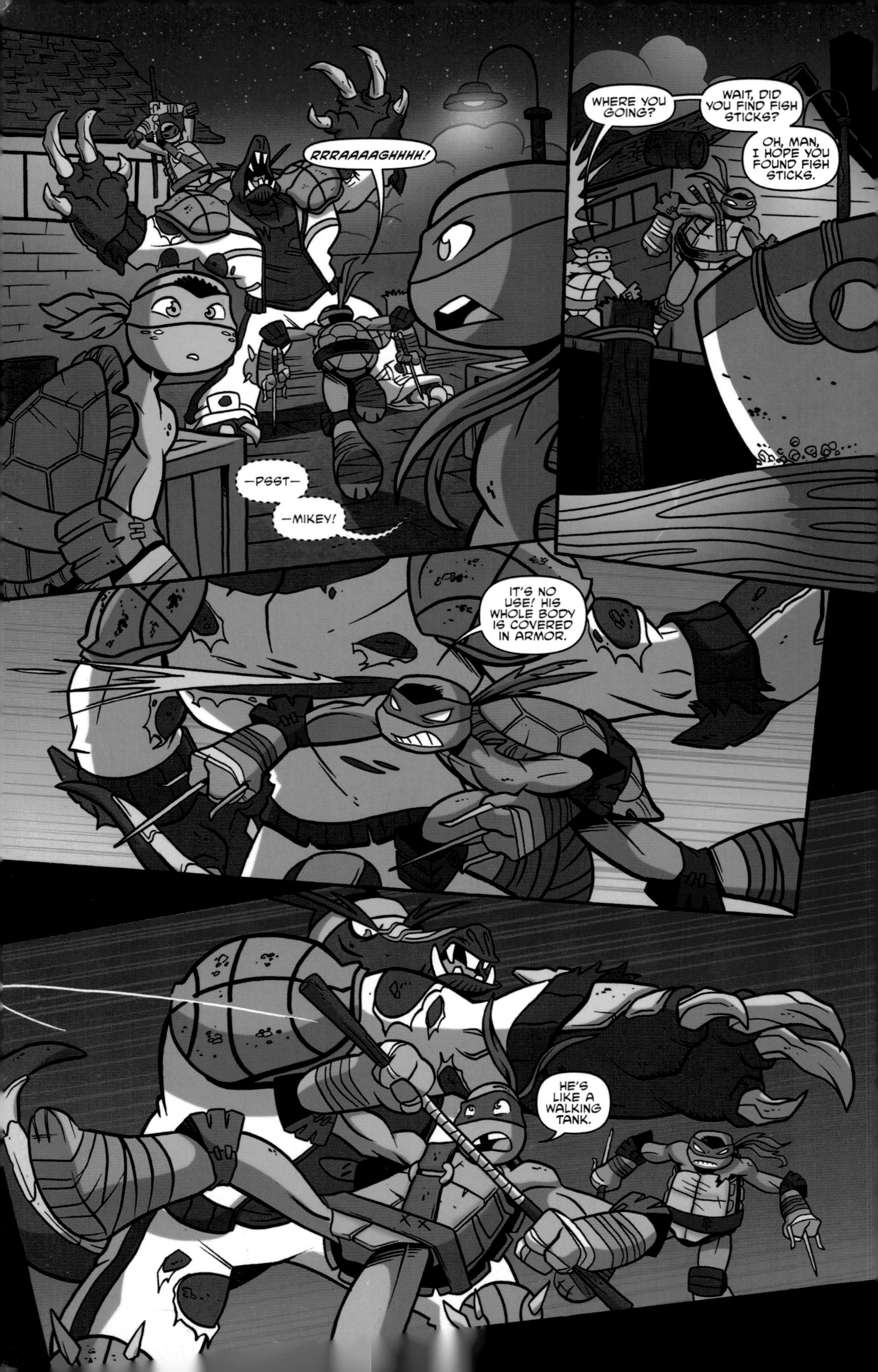
RRRAAAAAGHHHH!
—PSST—
—MIKEY!
WHERE YOU GOING?
WAIT, DID YOU FIND FISH STICKS?
OH, MAN, I HOPE YOU FOUND FISH STICKS.
IT'S NO USE! HIS WHOLE BODY IS COVERED IN ARMOR.
HE'S LIKE A WALKING TANK.

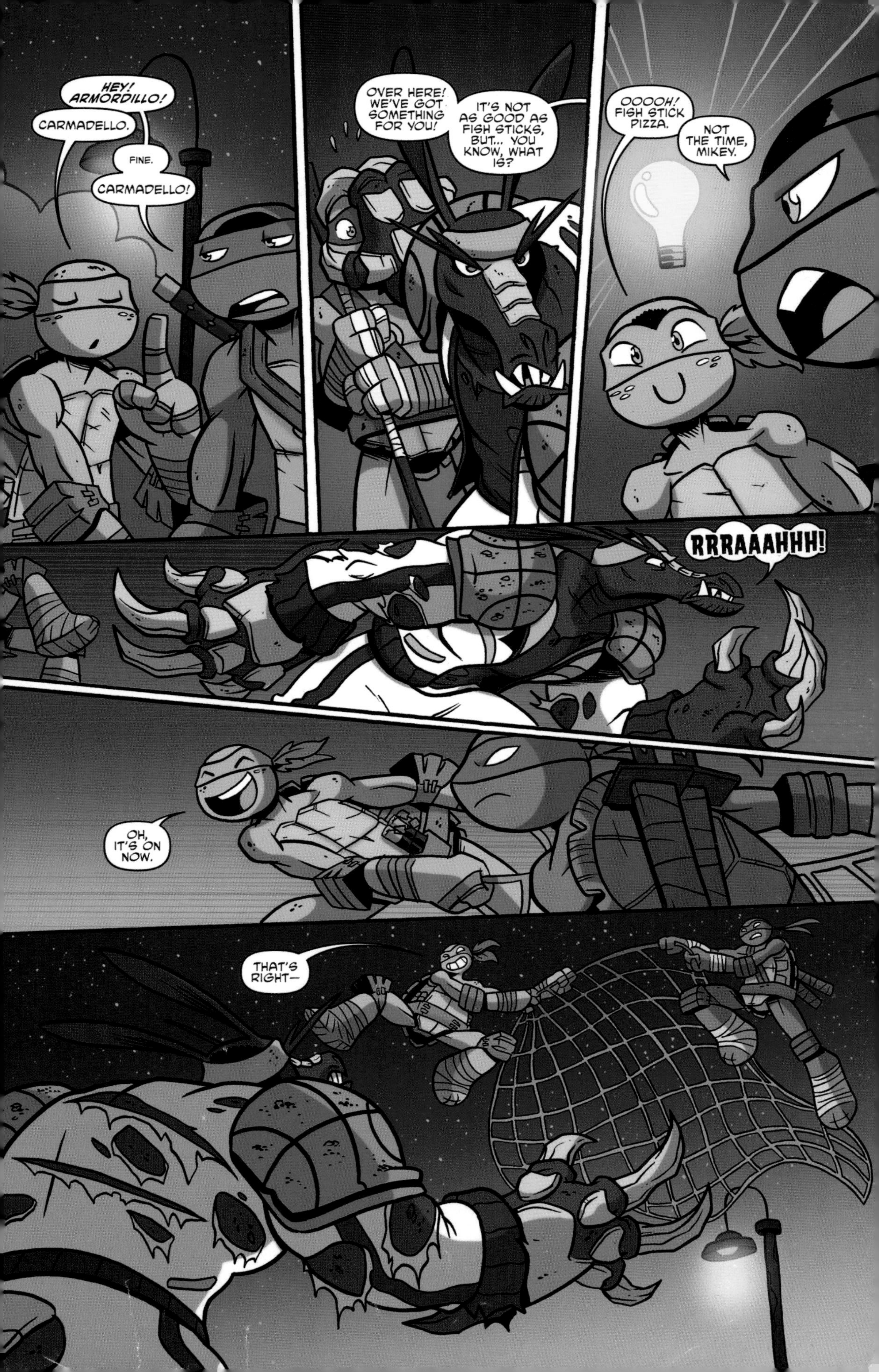
HEY! ARMORDILLO!
CARMADELLO.
FINE.
CARMADELLO!
OVER HERE! WE'VE GOT SOMETHING FOR YOU!
IT'S NOT AS GOOD AS FISH STICKS, BUT... YOU KNOW, WHAT IS?
OOOOH! FISH STICK PIZZA.
NOT THE TIME, MIKEY.
RRRAAAHHH!
OH, IT'S ON NOW.
THAT'S RIGHT—

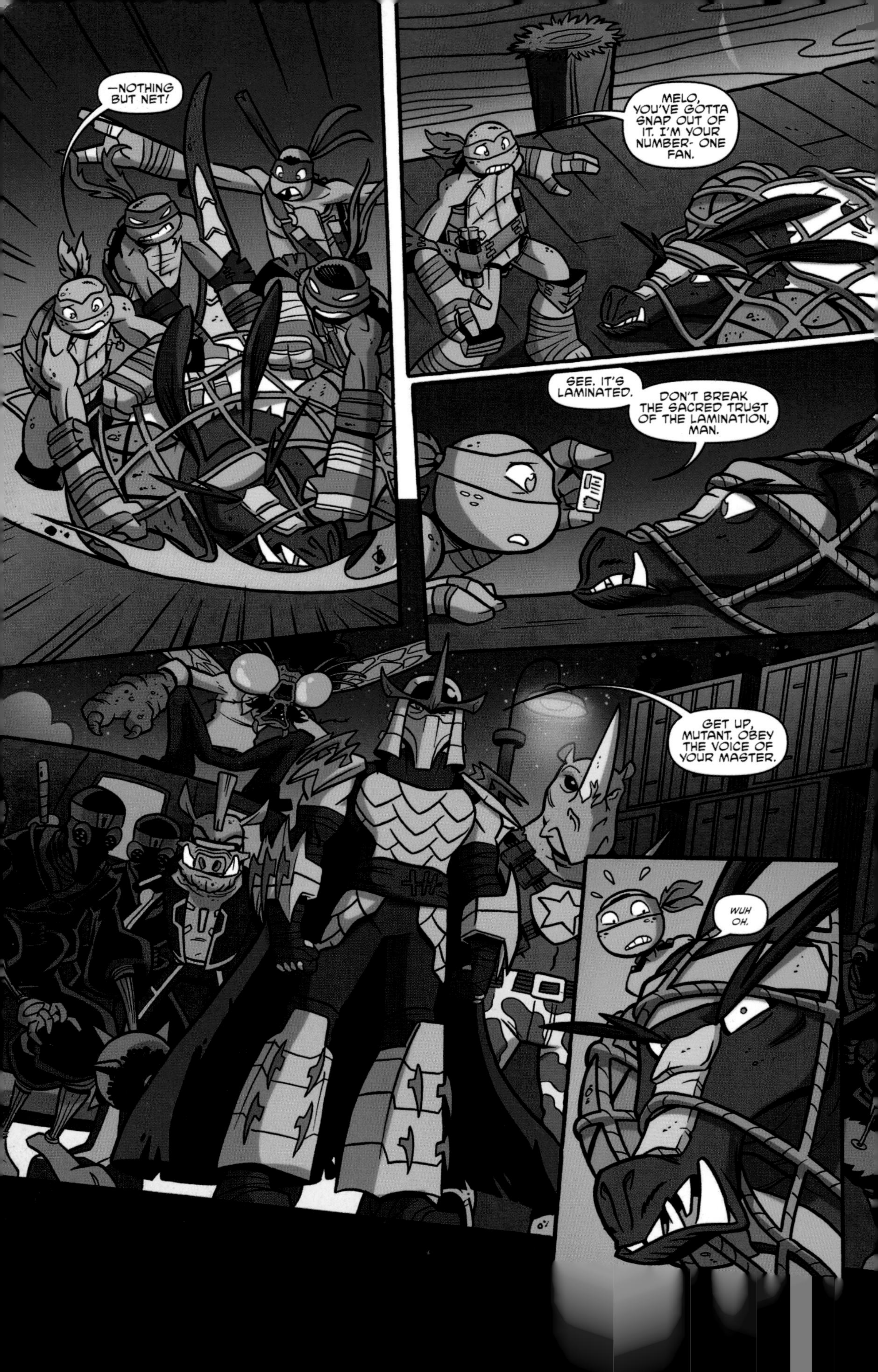
—NOTHING BUT NET!
MELO, YOU'VE GOTTA SNAP OUT OF IT. I'M YOUR NUMBER- ONE FAN.
SEE. IT'S LAMINATED.
DON'T BREAK THE SACRED TRUST OF THE LAMINATION, MAN.
GET UP, MUTANT. OBEY THE VOICE OF YOUR MASTER.
WUH OH.

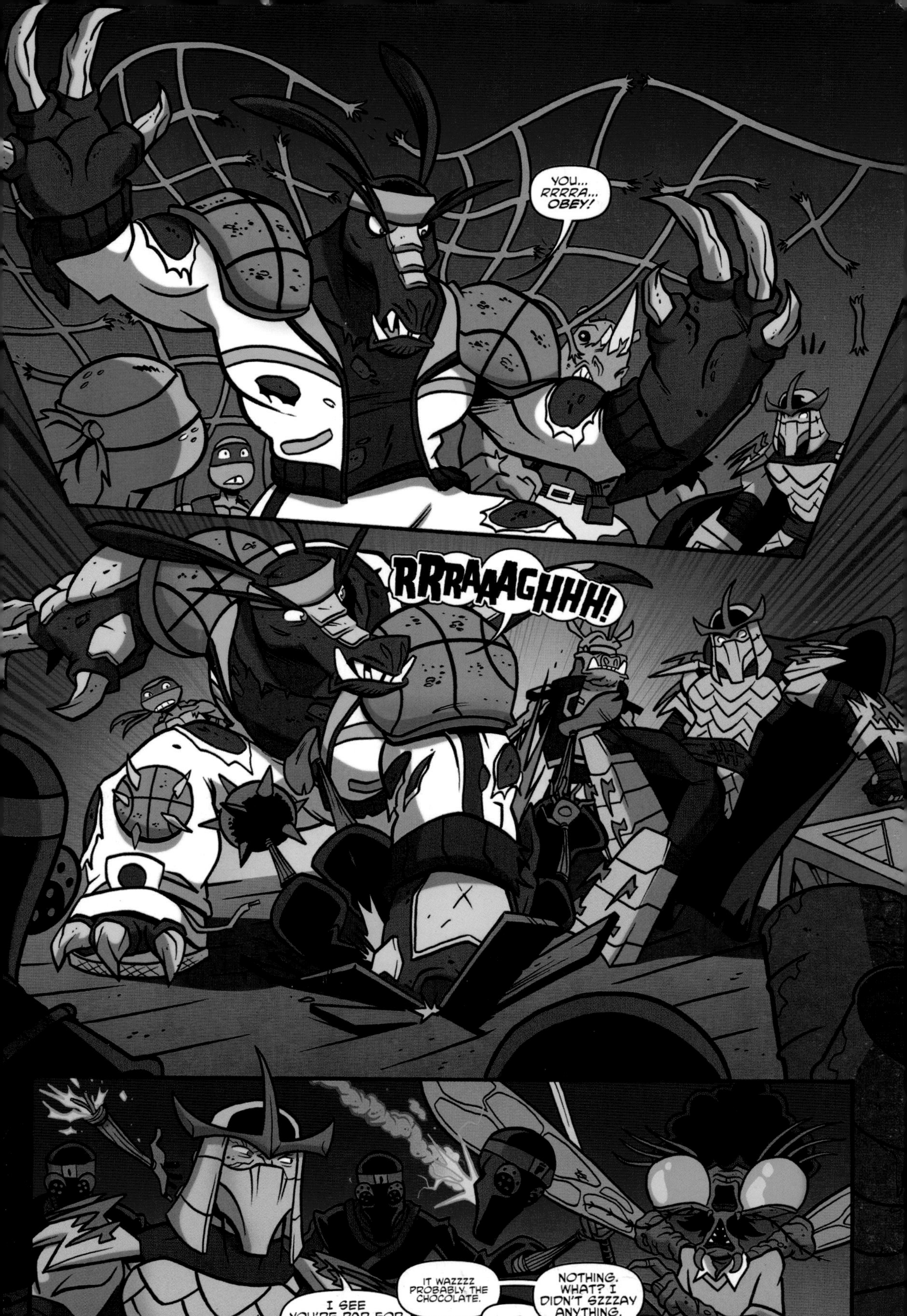
YOU... RRRRA... OBEY!
RRRAAAGHHH!
I SEE YOU'RE PAR FOR
IT WAZZZZ PROBABLY THE CHOCOLATE.
...?
NOTHING. WHAT? I DIDN'T SZZZAY ANYTHING.

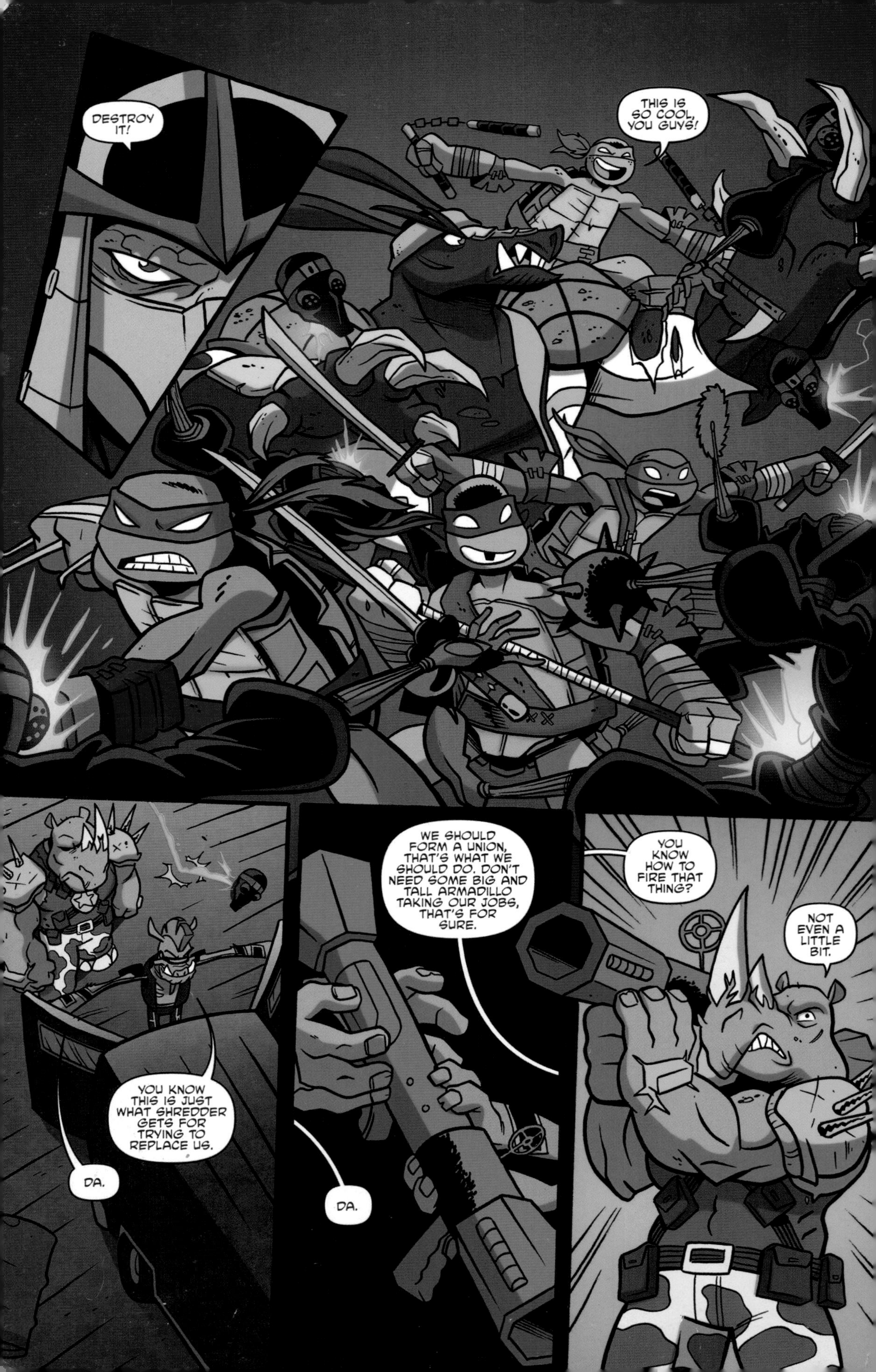
DESTROY IT!
THIS IS SO COOL, YOU GUYS!
YOU KNOW THIS IS JUST WHAT SHREDDER GETS FOR TRYING TO REPLACE US.
DA.
WE SHOULD FORM A UNION, THAT'S WHAT WE SHOULD DO. DON'T NEED SOME BIG AND TALL ARMADILLO TAKING OUR JOBS, THAT'S FOR SURE.
DA.
YOU KNOW HOW TO FIRE THAT THING?
NOT EVEN A LITTLE BIT.

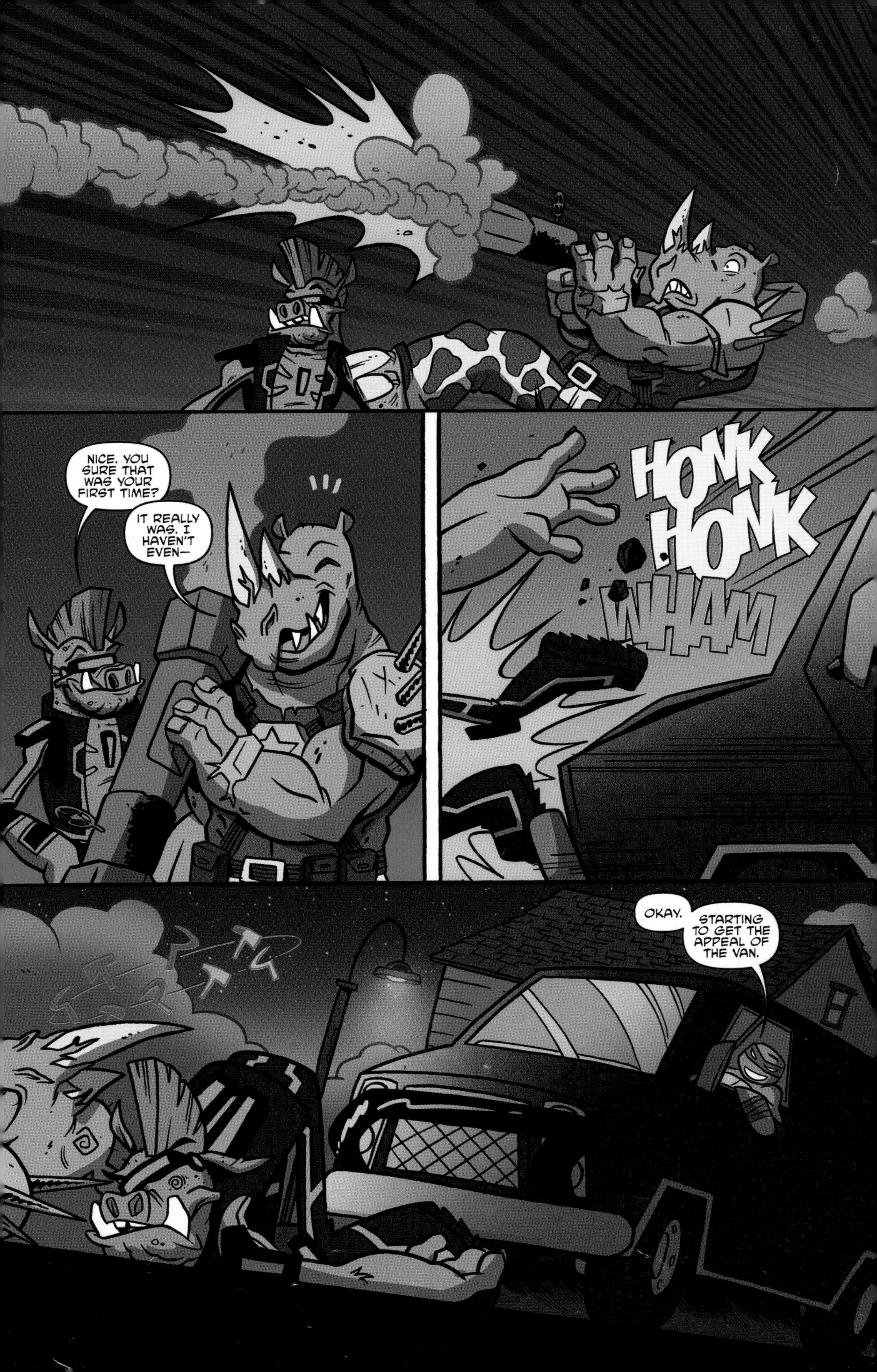
NICE. YOU SURE THAT WAS YOUR FIRST TIME?
IT REALLY WAS. I HAVEN'T EVEN—
HONK
HONK
WHAM
OKAY.
STARTING TO GET THE APPEAL OF THE VAN.

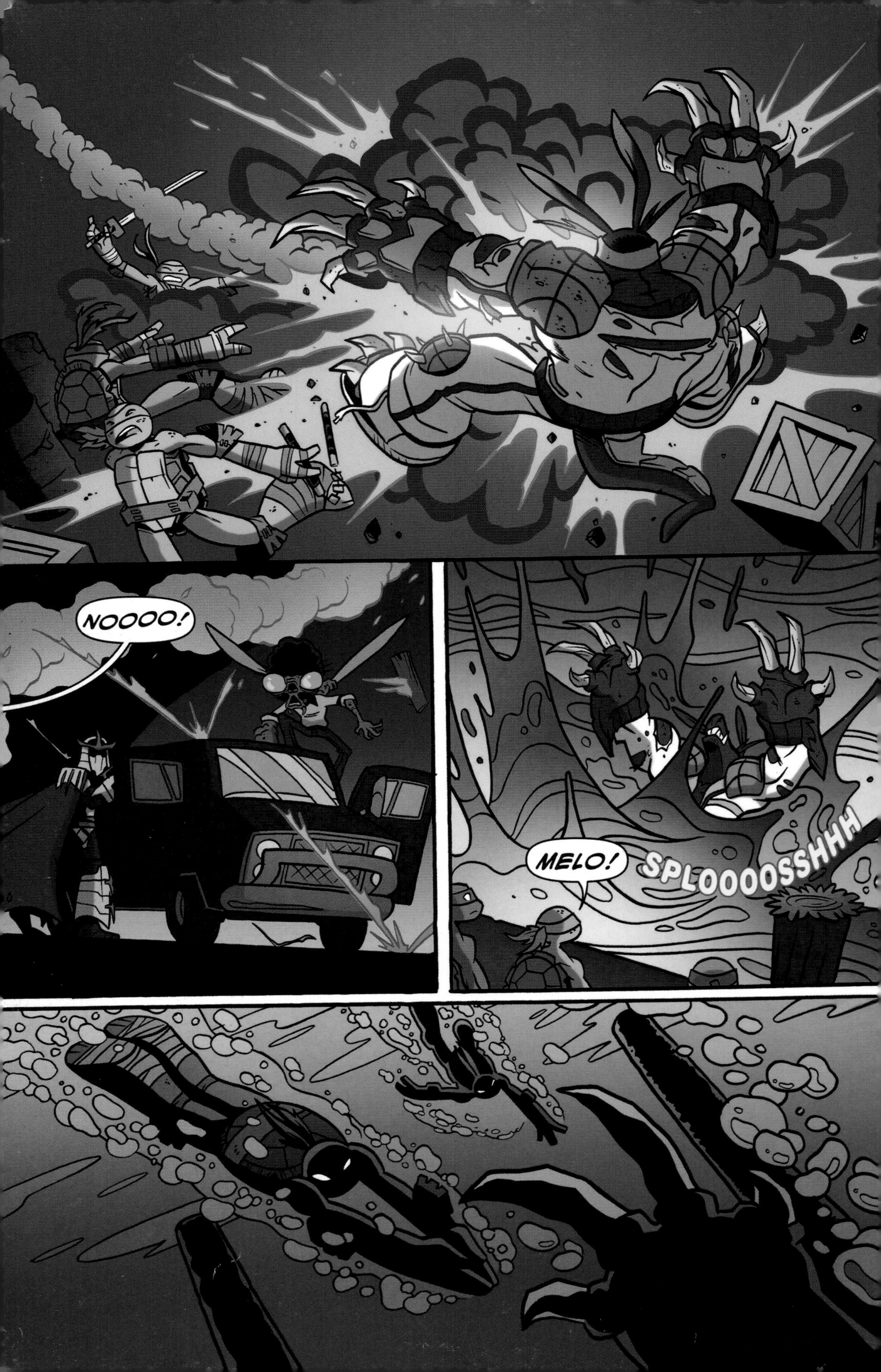
NOOOO!
MELO!
SPLOOOOOSSHHH

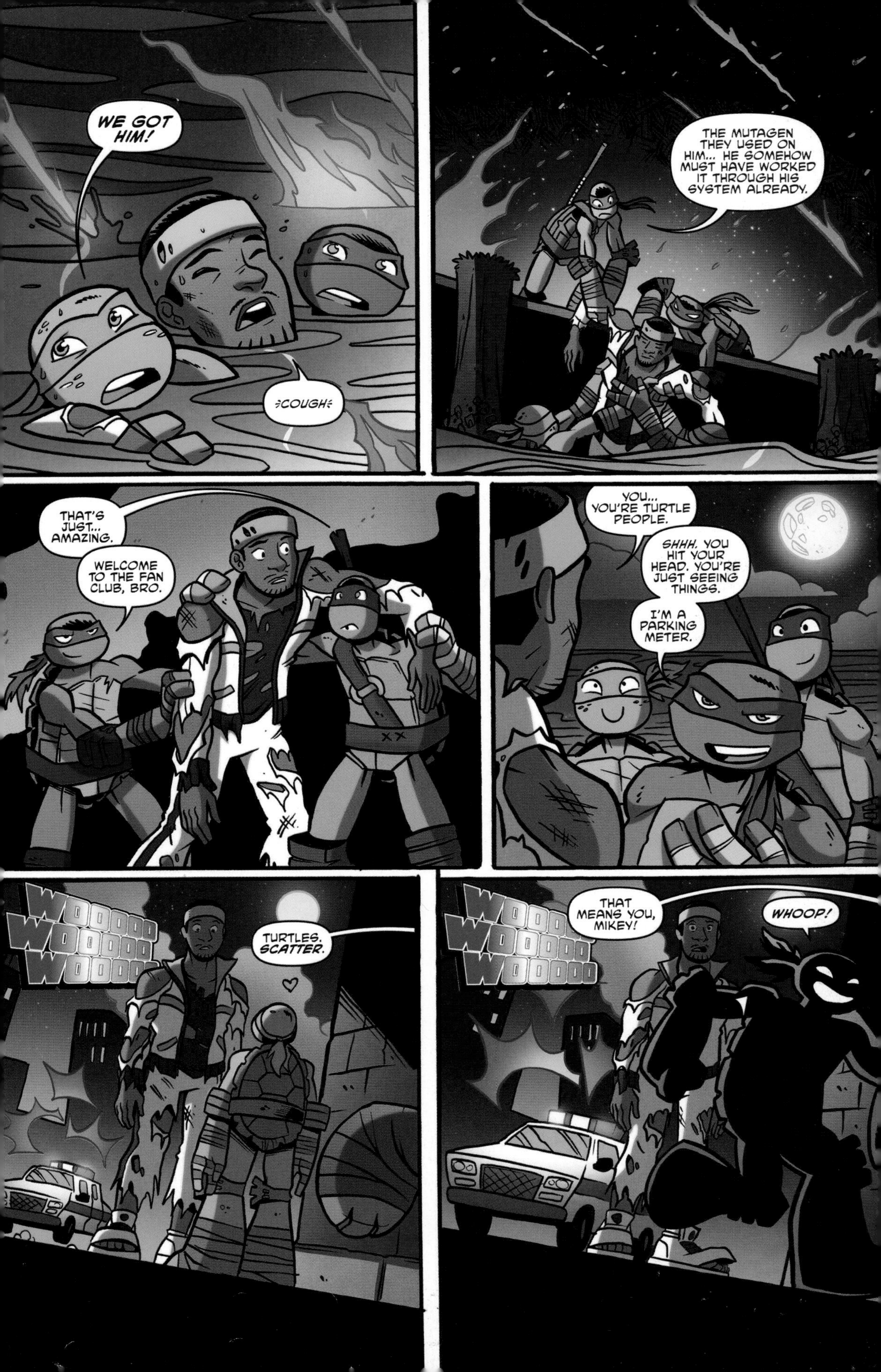

WE GOT HIM!
COUGH
THE MUTAGEN THEY USED ON HIM... HE SOMEHOW MUST HAVE WORKED IT THROUGH HIS SYSTEM ALREADY.
THAT'S JUST... AMAZING.
WELCOME TO THE FAN CLUB, BRO.
YOU... YOU'RE TURTLE PEOPLE.
SHHH. YOU HIT YOUR HEAD. YOU'RE JUST SEEING THINGS.
I'M A PARKING METER.
WOOOOO WOOOOO WOOOOO
TURTLES. SCATTER.
WOOOOO WOOOOO WOOOOO
THAT MEANS YOU, MIKEY!
WHOOP!

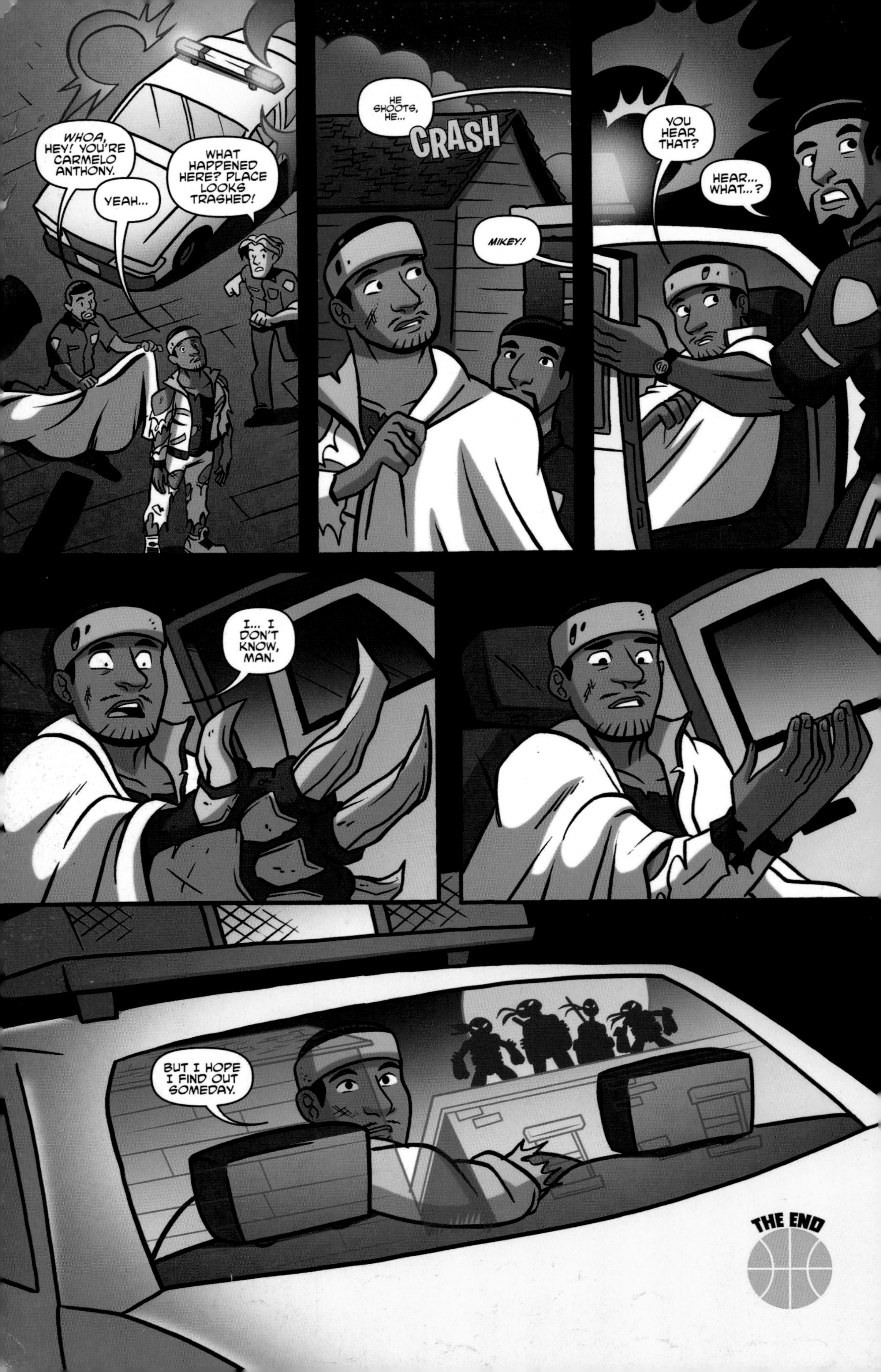
WHOA, HEY! YOU'RE CARMELO ANTHONY.
YEAH...
WHAT HAPPENED HERE? PLACE LOOKS TRASHED!
HE SHOOTS, HE...
CRASH
MIKEY!
YOU HEAR THAT?
HEAR... WHAT...?
I... I DON'T KNOW, MAN.
BUT I HOPE I FIND OUT SOMEDAY.
THE END

ART BY JON SOMMARIVA

ART BY JON SOMMARIVA

nickelodeon™

TEENAGE MUTANT NINJA TURTLES™

AMAZING ADVENTURES

VOLUME 4

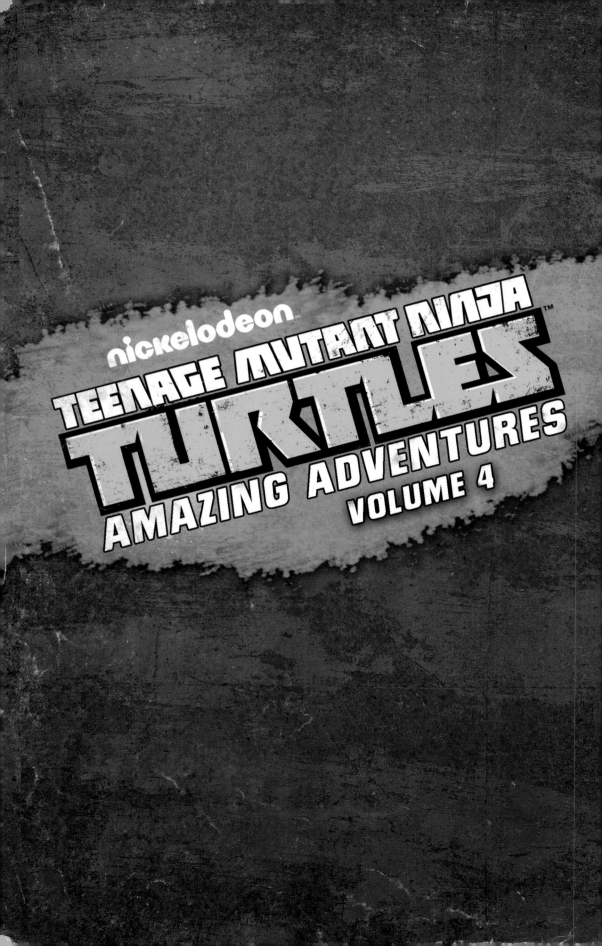